FORBIDDEN ALPHA BEAR

BRIDGE HOLLOW SHIFTERS 2

SAMANTHA LEAL

BOOKS IN THE BRIDGE HOLLOW
SHIFTERS SERIES

Alpha Daddy Bear (Book 1)
Forbidden Alpha Bear (Book 2)
Alpha Protector Wolf (Book 3)
Fated Mate Daddy Bear (Book 4)
Claimed by the Alpha Dragon (Book 5)

Forbidden Alpha Bear

Copyright ©2019 by Samantha Leal

All rights reserved. No part of this book may be reproduced in any form or by any electronic of mechanical means, including information storage and retrieval systems, without written permission from the author, except for the use of brief quotations in a book review. The unauthorized reproduction or distribution of this copyrighted work is illegal. No part of this book may be scanned, uploaded or distributed via the Internet or any other means, electronic or print, without the author's permission.

https://www.totallyromancebooks.com/samantha-leal

Join the Totally Romance Facebook Group!

CONTENTS

CHAPTER 1

$\mathcal{S}$cottsdale, Arizona

THE SUN WAS SETTING OVER THE HILLS AND CASTING A PINK and gold glow over the valley that sprawled out in front of him. The desert was dry and arid, but the colors that oozed from the ground were nothing short of spectacular. The purples and the oranges clashed together and produced something totally out of this world. Something that made Ernest stop and take notice, it truly made him appreciate all he had.

He sat and watched from the vista of his terrace, sat proudly in the large egg chair as he steepled his index fingers underneath his chin. Ernest would never get tired of this view, but the heat of the desert night, before the sun fully fell and plunged him into a familiar chill, wasn't doing anything to distract him from the rumors that had been heading out west to find him.

He had heard whispers of terrible things happening,

things people couldn't explain, and it was making him anxious and afraid.

He breathed in sharply and exhaled as his heart thumped away in his chest and his anxiety started to rise.

Ernest had been waiting for almost two weeks, but he knew he couldn't leave it much longer. Since he had heard what was happening in that little mountain town, it had done nothing but play on his mind.

He rose to his feet slowly and wiped his sweaty palms down the sides of his jeans, before he leaned over the balcony and looked out at the desert sand. He looked at the spindly trees and remembered still how lush and green a forest could be. He remembered the beautiful canopy of branches and leaves that surrounded Bridge Hollow, and for a brief moment, a smile flickered across his lips.

His stomach dipped and he shook his head before he turned away and headed back to the house. The bifold doors which extended the entire length of the backside were all open, letting in air and light but that meant he had to turn off the air conditioner, so when he stepped in, he felt the heat more than he had outside. He turned and began to close them one by one, and when he locked them, he slipped the key in his pocket and found himself looking around for anything out of place.

Ernest didn't know what could be lurking out there in the wilderness, and he didn't know if anything or anyone was coming for him, but he had to be mentally prepared.

He jumped as the hiss of the air conditioner started to blast from the vents that ran all along the top half of the room, and he felt the icy blast on his moist, hot skin, a welcome feeling.

He turned and walked down the crisp, immaculate, white tile and felt how cool it was underfoot. He passed by the rooms on each side of the hallway and marveled at the modern cleanliness of what was inside. Spotless living areas, black and white leather, modern artwork his assistant had furiously bid on for him at auction–which didn't serve much purpose now, but what would hopefully be a great investment and inheritance for his children sometime in the future.

Ernest had created himself a stunning oasis there in the middle of the desert, but lately, it had begun to feel more like a prison. He could feel what was coming, he knew a storm was brewing and he wanted to fight it before it had a chance to reach him first.

He peered through the pane of glass at the top of the front door and looked out across the driveway. His vast collection of cars was all in their own individual ports, already covered with protective blankets and put to bed for the night. Nothing stirred outside, but he still felt apprehensive, as if he could tell that he wasn't safe.

He checked the locks and then he lifted the receiver next to the main doorway which connected him to the security at the entry gate.

"Hello," he said as the guard answered. "I'm just checking we still have people patrolling the perimeter?"

"Yes, sir, we have a rotation and we've just switched, nothing to report so far."

The guard was stern and reassuring, and he hung up the receiver feeling better than before. He checked the locks once more and then he turned back and headed into the main body of the house again. The splendor rising around him, cocooning him and keeping him safe.

After the sun had set, and the night truly came in, he heard the howling of the coyotes out on the mountains. The valley was sprawling and wide, and he was perched right up at the top of it, a king surveying his own kingdom. But this time, he couldn't be present. All he could think about was

Bridge Hollow, of what he was hearing, of what could potentially be happening there.

He swallowed his nerves down and scratched the back of his neck, before he opened his drinks cabinet and reached for a crystal decanter that had long been hidden away but he could no longer ignore. He reached for a tumbler and poured in the whiskey, sloshing it around in the glass before he held it up to his lips and drank it down in one. The sensation of warmth and calm washed over him for a moment, but then his heart continued to race, and he poured himself another.

As he moved toward his desk, gripping the glass and raising it to his lips with shaking hands, he paused for a moment as he looked down at his computer.

He knew if he opened it, there would be no going back. All he would have to do was type the name of the town into a search engine and within seconds, he would have every conspiracy theory and latest news update known to man. With so much technology and information available at the touch of a button, there wasn't a place on Earth that Ernest could hide from this truth. And apart from that…

He had to know…

He sat down in his tall leather chair and slid under the glass desk, taking one last sip of the whiskey and draining his tumbler before he tapped the keyboard, the monitor of the computer blaring back to life.

He had spent so many nights alone, he had isolated himself from the world, and there was still no escaping it. He opened a search page and typed in Bridge Hollow, his fingers shaking with each tap of a key.

His eyes scanned the page, watching the results flash ahead of him. He saw the articles, some from only hours before, with various headlines all alluding to the same things…

· · ·

MISSING HUNTERS....
 MASS ANIMAL DIE OFFS...
 STRANGE WEATHER PHENOMENA...

AND HIS HEART BEAT EVEN HARDER BENEATH HIS RIBCAGE.

"Christ," he whispered as he rubbed his forehead and exhaled.

He knew it wasn't good. How could it be?

None of this was his fault, and yet, he had to know more. He couldn't help but wonder if any of this was relevant to him and his past...

He quickly clicked the X at the top of the screen and closed the page. He leaned back in the chair and steepled his fingers underneath his chin. He had sat on this for almost two weeks, but now that he had seen what the internet had to offer, he knew he was going to have to react.

His fingers grazed over the two files sitting in front of him. Two profiles of the people he was going to entrust. Ernest scanned the photographs pinned to the top of their identity documents and resumes, and his eyes stopped on the girl. He knew the man personally and had done for many years, but the girl was a stranger, someone selected for her knowledge and educational background. She was young and new to the field, recently graduated and coming with a set of fresh eyes. She didn't need to know the reason she was truly being sent to Bridge Hollow, and she certainly didn't need to know who she was working for.

He reached over to the phone sitting unassumingly on his desk and pulled the receiver up to his ear, the long wire trailing down almost to his knee. It was one of the oldest things in the entire building, but he didn't care. Why change something that would never be seen by anyone but him?

He flipped open his Rolodex and his fingers flicked through the pages until he stopped on one and bit his lip.

He didn't know if he was going to regret making this call, but he couldn't spend the rest of his life hiding up there in his gilded cage.

The ringing drilled away in his ear, and when he heard the click on the other end of the line his breath caught in his throat.

"Hello?" the voice sounded half asleep and dazed.

"It's me," he said. "Sean, I need your full attention."

The voice on the other end seemed to clear its throat.

"Yes, sir?" Sean replied, suddenly sounding a lot more awake than he had only a second before.

"I have something I need you to do," he said sternly. "Pack a bag and meet me at HQ."

"Yes, sir," the voice replied, clipped and military like.

He hung up the call and sighed, leaning back into his chair. The darkness seemed to be closing around him, just like the silence and sense of dread, but now, he would hopefully be setting the wheels in motion to bring him and everyone else back out into the light.

He spun around and looked out of the window behind him, at all the bright stars twinkling in the sky, at the deep, inky blue of the heavens and at the moon shining high above. He smiled.

This was his world, not anyone else's.

And he wasn't about to give it up without a fight.

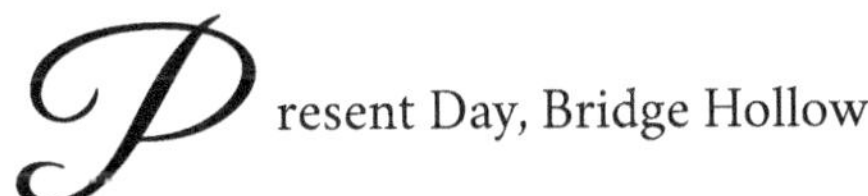

resent Day, Bridge Hollow

PAMELA LOOKED OUT THE WINDOW AS THE WORLD FLASHED BY her in a haze of green, brown and blue. The train was speeding across the country toward the mountains, and even though staring so intently at the scenery around her was making her dizzy, she couldn't help but be drawn to it.

The carriage was crowded and stifling, and she reached for the magazine that was laid face down on the table in front of her and began to wave it back and forth in front of her face like a fan.

She had spent the first couple of hours of the journey reading all about how to get that summer glow without actually having to sit out in the sun and expose your skin to harmful rays, she had read ten book reviews on the perfect beach reads, and she had perused articles on how to find the elusive G-Spot, all the while cringing at how predicable everything in this kind of mag was. Nothing was new and exciting any more, it was all the same stuff, recycled and churned out again and again every year.

She kept fanning her face, and with her free hand, she reached for her sparkling water and took a sip. At least the service on the train had been decent and she hadn't had to clash her way down to the bar cart and sit among god knows how many others trying to just pass the time and stay hydrated on what was starting to feel like a never ending trip.

Her colleague, Sean, sat in front of her and he glanced up momentarily and caught her eye. She smiled and looked away, but he sighed and placed the file he had been reading down on the table between them.

"I thought you might be excited rather than full of misery?" He said it with a wry smile, and she found herself rolling her eyes at him and grinning.

She had only known Sean for a few days, but already, his humor was beginning to rub off on her slightly. He was dry and witty, and even if they were sat in an overcrowded train cabin hurtling toward The Rockies, at least he was there to crack the odd joke and keep her sane.

"I know," she admitted, raising her hand and lowering the magazine in the other. "I can see that I haven't been the most enthusiastic companion."

Sean leaned across the table slightly and raised his eyebrows.

"That's an understatement," he said, before he leaned back and opened the file again, pulling it onto his knee.

Pamela had been casting her eyes toward the file, wondering what was inside and what information he had that she didn't.

Pamela had been hired by the government agency that Sean worked for only a month before, and now, she was out on her first job in the field, to investigate a series of strange environmental happenings in none other than the infamous Bridge Hollow.

When she had interviewed for the position she hadn't a clue what she would be doing on the job, only that they were looking for someone with as much experience as possible with the environment, geology, geography and science, and with her past degrees and PHD under her belt, Pamela had been the perfect fit.

She had spent her whole life preparing for this moment. Working hard at school and grad school, taking unpaid internships, and pulling some serious all-nighters. Her life was her career, and now, she had finally aced it by being hired by the government and pulled straight out into the field on a somewhat secret mission. But at this moment, her mission in life was to make sure that she did the best job possible and made the agency proud.

Sean cleared his throat and turned another page and Pamela watched him suspiciously. She wished she could see what he had in front of him, read what he was reading.

She was second-in-command to him. With Sean being the leader and the man in charge, he would be setting out and exploring more of the scientific side of things while they were in Bridge Hollow, and Pamela would be looking more at environmental factors. She closed the magazine-fan and placed it back on the table before she opened the lid of her laptop and pressed the power button so it came brightly to life. She was still new, and she didn't want to be seen as slacking, even if they were in the midst of one of the hottest days of the year, on a cramped train, with minimal air conditioning.

She waited for the computer to load and looked back to the window and at the scenery on the other side. The train seemed to have slowed slightly, and she smiled as she took in the lovely fresh greens and crystal-clear blue of the skies and lakes that weaved their way through the mountains below.

"Really beautiful, isn't it?" Sean said, breaking her concentration.

She nodded and smiled.

"Yes, it really is."

"Have you ever been out this way before?" he asked.

She turned to look at him and noticed that the file had been closed and placed back in his bag. She could see a set of documents peeking out the top, all the spines a crisp white.

"No," she admitted. "I've never been to the mountains before."

His eyes widened slightly, and he leaned in again.

"No way, you haven't even been skiing?"

"Nope," she half laughed and shrugged her shoulders. "I've always been too busy working my butt off and making sure I get where I need to be with my career to be taking vacations."

Sean cracked a smile and shook his head.

"Yeah, yeah," he said.

"It's true," she said smugly. "If I hadn't, then I wouldn't be sitting here today."

She crossed her arms over her chest and let her head lean against the side of the window. Her vision began to blur again, and she got swept up in the intense colors.

"Well, you're in for a treat then," Sean said as he rose to his feet and stretched.

She watched as he made his way down the aisle toward the doorway, clinging to the top of each seat as he passed.

When she was alone, Pam finally let herself breathe and relax. She was trying to be professional, but at the same time, Sean was so annoying she couldn't find it in herself not to slip into her regular girl mode and tease him a bit.

She took another sip of her water and looked down at

her watch. It was coming up close to 3pm and she knew the train was supposed to arrive in Bridge Hollow around half past. She had thirty minutes left on the sweltering train, and then, hopefully, she could disappear into this new little town and just be herself for a while before the working day began all over again and her and Sean would be back out on the job.

When the door between the carriages slid open and she saw him coming back down the aisle, she picked up her cellphone and pretended to be busy. She scrolled through social media until she lost signal, and she realized that they were heading up higher and higher into the mountains.

The small windows had been slid open slightly to let in some air, and the higher they climbed, the fresher it seemed to become.

"You smell the pine?" Sean asked as he sniffed in deeply. "Wonderful, isn't it?"

Pamela raised her eyebrows and nodded before she looked back down at her phone and closed the apps.

"What's the plan then?" she asked as she leaned forward across the table. "Are we heading out tonight or would you rather leave it until the morning?"

Sean reached up and ran a hand through his hair before he brought it back down and laid his arm along the full length of his bag, blocking her view of the files inside.

"I think we rest and go out at first light," he said, and suddenly, Sean the joker had disappeared and he was back to all business. "See what information we can gather at that time of day, and then stagger it out."

Pamela thought on what he was saying and nodded in agreement. He was right, if they were going to get a good cross section of what was happening in town, they were going to have to do the same tests at different times of the day, and what better place to start than at dawn…

"Okay," she said. "And what about getting around, do we have transport arranged or are we going on foot?"

Sean picked up his cellphone and tapped it to life. She saw him open an email and scroll through it.

"Transport will be there if we need it," he said as he shut the email down and smiled up at her. "You seem nervous."

The change of tone took her by surprise, and she found herself lost for words.

"This is your first time being sent out into the field," he said genuinely. "I get it, it is a bit nerve-wracking, but I wouldn't take it all too seriously, just do your job, gather what information you've been assigned to, and then, when it's all over, we get out of here and let the other's take over. Simple as that."

"Yeah...," Pamela said as she gazed back out of the window. "I know, you're right."

She saw the flicker of light in among the trees, as if the sun was catching on a pane of glass, and it was quickly followed by another. She sat forward and watched as a small smattering of log cabins came into view, followed by a long winding road, and then some other buildings. She cocked her head to one side and took it all in. Sean had been right when he said she was in for a surprise. The cabins and buildings all looked so quaint, like nothing she had seen before, and she could tell that this was just a taste, they were nowhere near the main hub of town.

"They look so cool," she smiled. "Like something out of a movie..."

The cabins began to fade into the distance, and she remembered the Christmas films she used to watch when she was younger. She always loved the idea of going out to the mountains with a big family, with a mom and a dad, a brother and sister maybe. But, in reality, all Pamela had ever known was her mom. She had been raised by a strong woman, she had never known her father, and for that reason, she had all but sworn off men. She had seen the heartbreak that had come from a man leaving her and her mother behind, and she was determined that it would never happen to her. And she certainly would never put a child through it.

It was the main reason she had focused so much on her career. She found that the more time and attention she gave to pushing forward with her education and then her work life, that she didn't have time to even think about meeting men anyway. And she, for one, was glad of it.

Some more cabins flashed into view and she felt a pang of want, which she quickly buried. It had been a childhood fantasy and nothing more. Now that she was in her mid-twenties, there was no way she was going to let herself be sucked back into the fairy tale ideal that was shoved down girls' throats since the second they opened their eyes.

There was no such thing as a prince to come and save them, and the perfect nuclear family was surely all but dead.

She felt herself grumbling and closed her eyes.

She couldn't let her past keep creeping up on her like that. She had her first serious job, and just because she was going out to a mountain town, which was completely new and unfamiliar, didn't mean she had to worry like she was.

She glanced down at her hands crossed in her lap and smiled.

She had already come a long way, and she had proven herself successful, now a big government agency had seen her worth too, and she was going to smash it.

She pushed her insecurities to the side as the train glided into Bridge Hollow. This was a new chapter for her, and she was determined to enjoy every moment.

CHAPTER 3

As the private car made its way out of the train station and into the main stretch of town, Pamela couldn't help but stare out the windows with wide eyes.

If she had been impressed by the look of the mountains and cabins on the journey in, then the actual town itself was like that but amped up to the max. The buildings were almost like gingerbread houses from the fairy tales she had read when she was a child. They were wooden, with red and green painted windowsills, some had thatched roofs, and others were decorated with hanging baskets of multicolored flowers and twinkling lights. It reminded her so much of Christmas and Easter together, but in the middle of the summer months, and everything seemed to have the most welcoming vibe to it, that she already felt completely at home.

She watched the people of the town conversing with each other. She saw the way they all smiled, how they walked with a spring in their step, how they all seemed to know each other. Coming from a big city, Pamela had never seen anything like this before, she was more used to avoiding eye contact and being shoved aside on the subway.

Bridge Hollow was cute, and she was looking forward to exploring this place and learning a lot more about it.

"Not what you were expecting?" Sean asked, clearly aware of the look of delight on Pamela's face.

"No," she laughed. "I guess not."

"The legends and rumors about this place," Sean snorted and rolled his eyes, "I mean, they must have some real nutjobs around here desperate for this place to be a tourist destination. But I guess they have to earn a living somehow…"

Pamela shot him an annoyed glance and leaned forward.

"What do you mean?" she asked. "Surely, there must be something behind it, no smoke without fire or whatever you want to call it."

Sean shrugged his shoulders and instantly looked disinterested.

"I'm here to prove fact," he said sternly. "I'm a scientist, not a fantasist."

She found herself looking completely in the other direction and rolled her eyes herself. She had heard plenty about the town of Bridge Hollow before she took the job at the agency, but since she had been assigned this task, she had looked it up even more and had been surprised by what she had found.

There were deep legends that spanned back decades. Details online were vague, but she had found a few forums where fanatics had been discussing the ins and outs of the town, and it had sparked her interest. She liked the fact that there were so many people determined that the legends were true. She read about the sightings of strange bear like creatures, or huge wolves and other monsters lurking in the forests and mountains around town. The place had become famous for it, and the tourists had flocked there every year, all year round, to try and catch a glimpse of one of the infamous and elusive monsters. It had become so popular a legend that the town even had an annual festival where hundreds of people would gather and celebrate all things magical and mystical, of all the legends and crazy stories that surrounded those woods and the land around it. When Pamela had read about it, she couldn't help but be drawn in and found herself wishing that she would be around to see it happen, but her assignment should be over long before the festival rolled into town, and she would just have to search for videos and pictures online to feel as if she had experienced it herself.

The car slowed and she turned back to the right to see it pulling up outside a large building. She ducked her head a little, so she could see out the window and read the sign on the front...

THE HOLLOW HOTEL

SHE WAITED FOR THE DRIVER TO STOP AND THE ENGINE WENT quiet. Sean opened his door and jumped out into the evening sun, and Pamela followed him, before the driver closed the doors behind them and went to the trunk to get their bags.

The hotel looked big and old, but it was clear that it had been recently refurbished. When she had done her searching online, she had discovered it was the only hotel in town, and for that reason, they clearly were not short on customers. She grabbed the handle of her wheelie case and made her way to the front door, with Sean at her heels. The doors slid open and she stepped into the quaint and charming lobby.

Ahead of her, a huge staircase seemed to cut the atrium in

two, it went up and onto the second floor, with the balconies of the floors above winding around and up to the top of the building.

Sean took the lead and made his way toward the reception desk, and Pamela found herself looking from left to right and at the two rooms that fed off from the reception. On one side was what looked to be a library bar, with books lining the walls and several people sitting and enjoying a cocktail hour drink in the dusky light. To the other side, she saw the waiters and waitresses setting tables for dinner, the scent of home cooking was wafting from the kitchen behind.

"Hello," Sean said with a sigh as he approached the desk and it became apparent that there was no one there.

Pamela watched him with a smirk as he undid the button on his shirt and ran a sweaty hand through his hair. It had been hot on the train and even though they had been sitting in the air-conditioned town car since they had arrived, it was clear that Sean had yet to cool down.

He breathed heavily out his nose and rubbed his temples before he leaned over the desk and started to tap his fingers on the wood.

"Hello?" he said again, his irritation clear for Pamela to see.

She cringed inside and hoped that whoever came out from the saloon doors behind the desk was ready for what Sean was going to throw at them, because she had the terrible feeling it was going to be one hell of a bad attitude.

"Hello?" he said again as he peered behind, clearly able to see that someone was there.

Pamela stepped up to stand behind him and wanted to intervene, but didn't see the point, he was her boss after all. If he wanted to act like a jackass, then she may as well let him. It wasn't going to do her any favors stepping up and telling him to calm down.

Behind the doors, a large shadow appeared, and then, they quickly swung open. Sean instinctively took a step back and cleared his throat nervously, and Pamela heard the heavy boots of whoever had emerged from behind reception stomp out before the sound of a big pair of hands slapped down on the desk.

Sean took another step back and Pamela looked up.

She felt her mouth sag open as she saw the man standing in front of them. She didn't know what she had been expecting from a hotel like this in the middle of a quiet town, but it certainly wasn't what was in front of her at that very moment.

Her heart began to beat fast and she felt herself become nervous. The man was tall and muscular, so tall, his head almost grazed the ceiling of the tiny reception area. He leaned forward, eyeballing her and Sean with menace.

"What?" he said so curtly it was almost like a bark.

Pamela's eyes grew even wider.

She couldn't help but let them travel around him. She went from the top of his head and his dark, rusty hair, down to his broad and tanned shoulders and down his incredibly big and powerful looking arms. He was like a brute standing there, and so completely out of place she didn't know if he had just robbed the place and they should call the police.

He looked more like a felon than a receptionist, and she could tell that Sean was feeling uneasy too.

The man looked from Sean over to Pamela and she saw his head cock slightly when their eyes met. It was so slight that if she hadn't been staring directly at him, she was certain she would have missed it. But when he saw her, it was as if she had taken him by surprise.

"So…," the man said, trailing his eyes slowly away from Pamela and back to Sean. "Are you going to tell me what is so important that you can't wait two minutes for my aunt to get back from the ladies' room?"

He crossed his huge arms over his shoulders, and Pamela was completely lost in his eyes. They were so dark and engulfing, she was transfixed. Whoever he was, he was clearly angry with them both, and he had instantly recognized Sean's irritated tone when he had barged into the hotel and wanted immediate service.

"I...we... emmm...," Sean stammered, and he scratched the back of his neck. "I just want to check in."

"Well, then, wait your goddamn turn," the man said from under his hooded brow, and Pamela couldn't help but let a little giggle escape from her lips.

Sean looked flustered and was bumbling an apology, and the man glanced at Pamela and caught her eye again. She felt a rush of excitement roll over her, and he smiled back too. It was just a flicker, the quickest, smallest smile she had ever seen, but she saw it and felt it and it made her want more.

His eyes stayed fixed on her and she was sure she could feel something between them, something hot and powerful, and she lost herself for a moment, before she pulled herself away and looked down at the floor.

What was she thinking? She wasn't there to ogle at hot guys, she was there to work and make a good impression.

She turned her back and closed her eyes, as Sean continued to mumble his apologies and dug himself further into the hole.

"Can you not check us in? You don't work here?"

"No," the man replied without the slightest hint of amusement. "And when the lady that does gets here, I want you to treat her with perfect respect."

Out of the corner of her eye, Pamela could see Sean nodding and it made her smirk again, but this time, she wasn't about to let the handsome stranger behind the desk see her. She had to remain professional and not get involved.

"Oh, thank you, dear," a little voice came from behind the doors and an old lady emerged. She was short and chubby, with perfect silver hair, and she reached up and patted the man on the arm before he wrapped a protective arm around her shoulder and gave her a squeeze. Then, he stepped out from behind reception and kept his angry eyes fixed on Sean.

"If you need anything, give me a shout," the man said to the old lady, before he turned and gave Pamela the dead-eye as he moved toward the door.

She felt her heart crash and her skin prickle with dread. He must have thought she was as rude and obnoxious as Sean was, and she didn't want to be tarred with the same brush.

"Thank you, Ryder," the old lady smiled, "I will."

Ryder…

The name thundered around Pamela's mind and she found herself looking back over her shoulder at him as he approached the main doors and stepped out and into the dying sun.

When she finally gained her composure and looked back to the lady at reception, she could see the look of knowing in her eyes and she felt herself blush.

"My nephew," the old lady said with a wink. "He pops round to help me from time to time."

Pamela smiled and tried not to let Sean see that she was blushing, before she picked up her bag and pulled it away from the desk slightly.

Sean checked them in to their own rooms and Pamela was in a daze while it was all happening. She didn't hear a word that the lady said to them, or a word Sean said when he handed her the room key. All she could think about was

Ryder and the fact that when he looked at her, something strange had happened.

She wandered up to the elevator in a dream and when she found herself on the third floor, she dragged her case along in a daze until she found the number written on the key card. She stopped and slid it into the lock above the handle and when the little light shone green, suddenly, a wave of tiredness seemed to knock her off her feet.

She opened the door and stepped inside, flicking on the light switch and smiling as the room illuminated and came to life. It was a gorgeous room, one with big doors that opened out to a balcony and to the vista of the mountains beyond. The sun was setting and it was darkening with each passing second, but she could see that the town was still vibrant and full of life outside, with the lights of taverns turning on, the sounds of music thumping through the streets and the laughter of the tourists and town's folk rumbling around every corner.

She pressed her nose against the glass door and watched the scenes in the town below and found her eyes traveling up to the forest and the mountains. This place was so perfectly beautiful, it was hard to imagine such horrors happening there. Surely, there must be a chemical plant or something close by responsible for the mass die-offs of animals. She felt a sadness take hold. To think of this place being poisoned was devastating, and something she couldn't even bear to think about. She shook her head and took a step back, before she opened her suitcase and started to unpack her clothes into the old wooden closet.

CHAPTER 4

By the time she had showered, freshened up, changed her outfit into a cute pair of jeans and a skinny t-shirt and unpacked, it was getting close to 8pm. The town showed no signs of quieting down, and even though she had been tired, she now felt wide awake and eager to get out and see more of the place.

She looked at her cellphone and the screen flashed with a message from Sean…

S: I'M HEADING OUT TO FIND SOMEWHERE TO EAT, LET ME KNOW IF you want anything!

SHE STUDIED IT FOR A MOMENT AND SCRUNCHED UP HER LIPS. She had probably had enough of Sean for one day, and she knew they were going to be spending plenty of time together during the coming weeks, so she decided against taking him up on his offer and wrote a quick reply.

· · ·

P: Thanks Sean, but I'm going to head out myself and do a little exploring. See you in the morning, bright and early!

She hit send and slipped the phone into her purse and slung it over her shoulder before grabbing her jacket. She turned off all the lights, apart from the beside lamps and the room looked so cozy and welcoming, she almost couldn't wait to get back and climb into bed for an amazing night's sleep.

"But first things first," she said as she held back her shoulders and headed for the door. "Let's see what this place is all about."

As she wandered down Main Street, she was fascinated by the different groups of people, and at how much fun a small town seemed to be having out there in the middle of the mountains. She had read that Bridge Hollow was a tourist hotspot, but she had never expected it to be so full of skiers, holiday makers, and families having a great time together in the midst of so much rumor and legend.

She wandered past shops that were completely unique and rustic. She saw grocers selling Bridge Hollow's own label jam and bread, their own ale and cider, bottles of wine, cheeses that had been made from dairy farms close by, and many other gorgeous looking treats that she couldn't wait to devour. There was a mystical shop that had a bead curtain flapping in the breeze at the doorway and the strong smell of incense drifting out from the inside. A secondhand bookstore and coffee shop, handmade clothing and an expensive crystal wear store were all dotted across the street, and nothing seemed to be from a huge corporate chain, everything was completely unique and enchanting.

She stopped and peered through some of the windows as she passed by, but it wasn't until she came closer to the very center of Main Street that her mind was completely blown. She felt the tingles rush up her spine and prickle the skin on her arms as she stared up at the statue. Her mouth sagged open a little and she swallowed as she stared up at the bronze structure ahead of her.

It was big and unmissable, right in the center of town, and it gave her the shivers because of the look of rage and power etched on its face, but also because she knew it was in reference to one of the oldest legends of Bridge Hollow.

The statue she was looking up at was of a huge, hulking half man, half bear. It looked as if a bear was ripping out of a man's body, turning into the beast right there in the center of Main Street. The eyes of the bear were wild and unnatural, the look of pain and bloodthirst apparent, even though it was just a statue.

She shuddered.

"Wow," she whispered. "Impressive."

She stayed watching it for a few moments, and then the loud crack of a motorbike coming to life shook her out of her stupor and she turned to see a group of rough looking, leather-clad bikers all lined up on their Harley's outside of what appeared to be a bar.

The building was long and wooden, it looked big and cavernous through the windows. From the sounds coming from inside and shadows flashing across, she could already tell that it was well patronized for the evening. The bikers were leaving, but they all revved their engines as they shook each other's hands and prepared to get going, and a group of other men waited in the doorway to the bar and waved them all off as they went, one by one, revving and howling as they flew down Main Street in the opposite direction of Pamela.

She watched as the men in the doorway of the bar backed

inside and it half closed behind them, the rock music from within was still playing loudly and thumping out through the ground to where she was standing. Pam let her eyes travel up to the sign above the door and found herself frowning when she saw the name of the place was SHIFTER'S BLISS. It sounded so PG and family friendly, but with a gang of hairy and menacing bikers out the front, she could only guess it was anything but…

She shrugged her shoulders and felt a little grin creep across her lips. She may as well get herself in there and see what it was all about. It was her first night in a new town after all, and the more she learned before she started her job the following day, the better. Plus, she had to admit, she could kill for a beer.

She pushed the door open and stepped inside, where she was immediately hit with the hot smell of beer, wood smoke and meat. She hadn't realized that she was hungry, but the smell of the hog roast that was heavy in the air set her stomach growling, and her mouth began to water.

The bar was dark and crowded, with each table seemingly filled with groups or couples. A stage was dark, but still set at the front of the room, with guitars and drums, as if a band were going to be playing later in the evening. She looked ahead to the bar and at the high stools lining the front of it. She could easily hide away and slink into the one empty booth that appeared to be free at the back of the room, eat something quietly and then get herself out of there, but for some reason, she was feeling a lot more sociable than usual, and she wanted to enjoy her first night in town before all the hard work began.

She stepped confidently up to the long, wooden bar and sat down on one of the high stools, before she placed her purse down in front of her and instantly searched deep inside it for her phone so she had a prop to help keep her busy if she wasn't lucky enough to get chatting to one of the locals.

She glanced around herself and saw that a few seats down were a couple of old-timers, supping on Bridge Hollow's own beer and smoking rolled cigarettes, and she felt the urge to smile and go speak to them, but knew she had to resist.

She had watched plenty of TV shows to know that this was the kind of place she could hear plenty of gossip about what was happening there in town, but what she was most intrigued to know was if there was some kind of chemical plant that had been hidden off the radar that might slowly be poisoning the land around them. She had heard of hidden facilities before, ones that were privately funded, that were dabbling in questionable activities and maybe even testing on animals. If something like that was happening in such a beautiful place, never mind so close to a national park, then there was going to be one hell of a big lawsuit going down, and heads, for sure, were going to roll.

She tried to listen in on their conversation, but the noise around her was too loud, and she quickly gave up and turned back to peer into the refrigerators behind the bar, scanning them for something to drink. When the girl who was serving finished with her customer, she glanced in Pamela's direction and wandered over to her with a smile.

"Hey there," she said cheerfully. "What can I get you?"

Pam held out her hand and waited for the girl to shake it, which she finally did, suspiciously, and cocked her head to the side.

"Hi," Pam beamed. "I'm Pamela, I've just got into town."

"Oh yeah?" the girl grinned and seemed to relax. "And how are you finding it so far?"

"Great," she said. "It seems like a friendly little place."

"It sure is," the girl nodded. "I'm Wendy, here to serve all your drinking needs."

Pamela laughed. Wendy looked like a nice girl and couldn't have been much older than herself.

"Well, in that case, I would love to try one of these Bridge Hollow beers," Pamela said as she looked back down to the row of them sitting and glinting under the light of the refrigerator.

"Sure thing," Wendy smiled as she reached down and collected one before she snapped off the cap and passed it across the bar top.

"Thank you," Pamela said, before she raised the bottle to her lips and took a sip. She had always liked beer, but this one seemed different, it was smoother and less bitter, light and airy, much like the mountain air. "Wow," she grinned. "That's good."

"It is, isn't it!" Wendy smiled and laughed. "I love it too, definitely a good one for us girls to enjoy."

"I was just thinking the same thing," Pam agreed.

"One of the families in town makes it up on their farm," Wendy continued. "They brew it all themselves and it goes down really well with the tourists. Are you here for the last of the ski?" Wendy's eyes were deep blue and kind, and Pamela instantly felt at ease around here.

"Actually, no," she admitted, gliding into conversation with Wendy without fear and glad that she finally had someone to chat to instead of Sean. "I'm here for work."

Wendy raised her eyebrow.

"Oh really?" she asked with interest. "What kind of work?"

"Environmental," Pamela nodded. "The company I work for has sent my colleague and me here to investigate the strange weather and animal activity."

Wendy smiled a wry smile and nodded slowly.

"It's been a strange couple of months," she seemed to agree. "A lot of people around here would love to know what is going on. Especially, regarding the two hunters that went missing up on the mountain."

"I heard about that," Pam continued. "Seems like a lot has been going on here."

"Oh, when doesn't it!" Wendy laughed.

A man down the other end of the bar leaned over and began to call her, tapping on the countertop and motioning with his wallet that he wanted to buy some drinks.

"I better serve him," she smiled, "if you want anything else, just give me a shout."

Pamela nodded and watched as Wendy moved down to serve the other customers, then she relaxed against the back of the stool and took another sip of her beer.

She liked it in Shifter's Bliss. It was raw and edgy, full of a wild mix of people, but welcoming and warm. She could hear the logs snapping in the little fires that were lit in the firepits, and she looked around, trying to figure out where the kitchen or smell of hog roast was coming from. She pulled a menu to her and started to flick through it. The pages were wrapped in plastic, no doubt to protect the paper from spills from the drunks as they drooled over the pictures when they were looking for snacks to go with their booze. As she flicked through, she noticed that in corner of each page was the image of a bear, and it didn't take her long to recognize that it was the same snarling face from the statue in the center of town.

She closed the menu and slid it slowly away from here and took another swallow. This was such a strange little place, full of quirks and in its own little world.

She heard a roar of laughter coming from behind her and she turned to look over her shoulder to see the group of men who had been standing in the doorway when she arrived to wave off the bikers. They were all gathered in one of the booths that lined the back wall, and it looked like they had been there for a while, with huge empty glasses scattered around the table, empty bottles of beer and a half-full bottle of whiskey. They were clearly all very merry, some of them roughhousing with each other. Two of them got up and went to sit at a clear table next to the booth and started to have an arm wrestle.

She laughed to herself a little and kept watching, until she felt the eyes of someone from the group on her and she let hers meet with them.

When she saw who was watching her, her heart almost stopped in her chest and her skin began to prickle.

His eyes were deep and dark but fixed intently on her from across the room, with a look of trouble on his face, as if he were half angry, and half unsure of what he wanted to feel.

It was the man from the hotel.

Ryder.

Instinctively and out of shyness, Pamela quickly broke eye contact and looked away. She turned back to face the bar and took a deep breath.

Oh my god, she thought. *It's him...*

She sipped her beer and tapped her cellphone to bring it to life, suddenly feeling as if she were very much on display. It didn't matter that the bar was crowded, and that most of the people in there were either drunk or too involved in their own conversations to notice her. Now that she knew Ryder had spotter her, she knew she wasn't going to be able to rest.

She opened her emails and started to flick through them, trying to take her mind off the fact that one of the most handsome and sexiest men she had ever seen, and had subsequently been given a seriously nasty look from a few moments later, was right behind her.

She loaded one of the PDFs from an email and scanned through it, not taking any of it in. She saw words like *soil, minerals, ph levels...* and as her eyes flickered down the page, she felt them start to water and her vision started to blur.

She looked up and away from it, ready to try and catch Wendy's attention, when, to her complete shock and surprise, Ryder came out of nowhere and stepped behind the bar himself.

His eyes were still fixed on Pamela, but his expression had softened slightly. She smiled weakly at him and then looked nervously away, hoping that he wasn't about to lay into her for what had happened back at the hotel.

"Hey... again...," he said as he reached down to the refrigerator and pulled out a bottle of beer. He snapped off the cap with his teeth and blew the bottle top into the trash. He made it look so effortless and easy, it took Pamela by surprise and she was lost for words.

"Hi," she finally managed to whisper, hoping that a ferocious blush wasn't spreading out across her cheeks and entire face.

"So, did you and your boyfriend get checked in?" he asked her, a cloud turning his face to stone.

"He isn't my boyfriend," Pamela found herself snapping back. "But yes, thank you, we did."

He smirked and raised the bottle to his lips and took another drink.

"Listen," Pamela interjected before he had chance to speak again. "I'm sorry for the way Sean was back at the hotel, I want you to know that I don't condone him or his behavior."

"Well, why would you?" Ryder raised his eyebrows. "He's a total jackass. And like you said, he's not your boyfriend, so you don't need to apologize."

He grinned at her, as if he was trying to get her to bite.

She narrowed her eyes and smirked back.

"I just wanted you to know, we're not all like him."

"What, tourists?" he half snorted. "Well, I know that."

"No," she laughed. "Scientists."

Ryder's eyebrows raised much like Wendy's had done and she watched as he set the bottle of beer down and crossed his arms over his chest defensively.

"And what is a scientist doing in this town?" he said with an underlying challenge.

"For work," she said matter-of-factly.

Ryder ran his tongue under his lip and across his teeth while he kept his eyes fixed firmly on her. The way he was looking at her was unnerving, it was almost like he was hungry, and she was his next meal. But there was something so standoffish about him too, as if she were annoying him by just existing. She knew she was babbling and not acting herself, so she looked away and took another sip of her drink.

Ryder reached down and opened the refrigerator before he pulled out another bottle and set it in front of her. She looked up into his eyes again, and she felt something move inside her heart. He was closer to her than he had been back at the hotel, and she felt a pull toward him. Her spine tingled and she felt hot all over, right under her skin and creeping up her neck. Her heart beat faster and she was sure that something gold glistened in the middle of his eyes.

"Here," he said. "Have this on me. Welcome to Bridge Hollow."

He smiled and snapped the cap off with an opener, slid the bottle right in front of her and stepped away. She watched him move behind the bar and off into the throng of waiting customers. He began to serve them, pouring drinks quickly and smashing open the register with his big, heavy hands.

Pamela couldn't take her eyes off him, she was completely entranced. Who was this guy? Did he work there, doing odd jobs and moonlighting at the hotel to help his aunt, or was he something else?

She watched him out of the corner of her eye and tried not to let him see, but on a few occasions, he looked up at her and she had to turn away.

Finally, after what seemed like a decade, Ryder strolled back to her end and leaned back against the far counter, drying clean glasses with a cloth and stacking them up in neat piles.

She looked up and watched him and he smiled at her again.

"So, I take it you work here then?" Pamela asked when she worked up the courage.

He was barely even three feet away from her, but she could still feel a heat between them, as if there was a chord tugging them together.

He nodded slowly and then his eyes met hers again.

She felt a jolt, as if she were becoming addicted to looking into his eyes and she had just gotten a fix. They were so dark and enchanting, and the gold shimmer deep inside of them, just around the pupil, was mesmerizing her and making it impossible for her to look away.

"Yes," he said, "I own the bar."

His voice was deep and gruff, and he had a confidence about him that was completely arousing. She cleared her throat and looked down at her knees, hoping she still wasn't blushing.

"Cool," was all she could manage to say.

He owned the bar she was sitting in… what were the chances? Only a few hours in town and she had already invaded this guy's peaceful evening twice.

He smiled and picked up another glass and kept drying it.

"Who were the bikers?" she asked suddenly, to try and change the subject.

Ryder's eyes widened a bit as if he were impressed.

"Are you sure you're a scientist and not an investigator?" he asked with amusement.

"I guess there's not a whole lot in-between," she said.

He smiled and his demeanor softened slightly.

"Just some guys we know," he said. "Don't worry, they're harmless. I'm sure they have nothing to do with whatever you're here to look at."

"The strange weather and the die offs?" she blurted out.

She knew she had already tested the water with Wendy, but she had not stopped working since, and it was clear that if Ryder owned the bar, he would be more inclined to sit and chat with her.

He smiled again and then turned his back on her and reached down for another beer.

"Here," he said as he passed it to her and set it down on top of the counter. "Enjoy, again, on me."

He didn't say another word, but he stepped out from behind the bar and disappeared back toward the crowd of men who were drinking in the back booth. She looked casually over her shoulder and saw him sit among them and get back into conversation, and she wondered why people seemed to be shutting down whenever she mentioned why she was there.

She raised the bottle to her lips and took another sip before she yawned and looked at her watch. It was only 9:30pm, but she knew she had a busy day ahead of her, and she didn't want to risk any kind of hangover by sitting in Shifter's Bliss for too long, drinking the night away with the locals.

She thought back to the way Ryder had spoken to her. How she felt something when she looked into his eyes, and even now, as she sat there, she could feel him watching her. It was as if she could sense him when he was near, and they couldn't help but be drawn to each other, but she also knew she had drank three beers and hoped that it was just a mild buzz washing over her and making her feel more carefree.

She opened her purse and pulled out twenty dollars and set it under one of the empty bottles. She picked up her things and gave Wendy a little wave as she turned and headed toward the door.

I don't need anyone's charity or a man to buy me drinks, she thought to herself as she walked past the table of rowdy men and felt Ryder's eyes still on her. Pulling her in and watching her every move.

When she reached the door, she finally looked up, and their eyes instantly met. Around her, the noise seemed to fall away, and for a split second, it was as if they were the only two people in the room.

Her heart raged in her chest and all she could hear was it beating, the pulse rushing through her veins getting faster as she looked into his eyes, wishing she could move closer.

She broke their connection and stepped out the door and into the night, and she had to take a moment to find her breath.

She had no idea who Ryder was, or what hold he had over her, but just being near him was sending her lust and mind into overdrive, and it was unnerving.

She composed herself before she rushed away from the door of the bar and as far away from him as she could. She glanced back over her shoulder and the door to Shifter's Bliss was empty, but she could still feel him, as if he were watching her from the shadows.

Back in the hotel room, she locked the door behind her and sighed, sitting on the bed. The curtains were still open to the doors to the balcony, and she could see the twinkling lights scattering up the mountain, and the sound of singing and laughter coming from one of the taverns down below.

She breathed in and out deeply and stared up at the ceiling. It had been a crazy day, and now she was overthinking even more about Bridge Hollow and what this place meant.

She thought of Ryder, her mind swimming with possibilities. It had been the first time ever that a guy had even caught her attention, let alone made her heart race and her head spin the way it was doing now. She had always managed to avoid being drawn to someone, but this felt different.

She remembered the intensity of his eyes, the way they had glistened with gold and seemed out of this world. She could have kept looking into them all night and gotten lost. She could have dived right into their depths and stayed forever, but there was something about him that was cool and aloof, and she didn't know what it meant.

She rolled onto her side and rubbed her forehead. She didn't even know what she was thinking getting herself all worked up like that.

"You're here to work," she whispered to herself, as if she was scolding a child. "You don't need a complication, or anything to make you look bad at the agency…"

She clamped her mouth shut as if she couldn't even believe she was saying the words out loud.

This is ridiculous, she thought. *You don't want a man, and you certainly don't want someone taking advantage of you and throwing you off you're A-game while you're here starting out your career.*

She could only imagine what her mother would be saying to her if she were there at that very moment. She would be furious with her, and she would be telling her, *Pamela hadn't come this far just to give it all up at the last moment for a quick fling with a hot mountain man.*

But god, was he hot…

He was nothing like the guys she had been warned about in her city back home. The kind of well-groomed city boys that she had known to avoid like the plague. She had only focused on her career, and she had always managed to stay well out of the dating game.

But Ryder, he seemed different.

Rugged and raw, and there was more to him, she could tell.

She shook the thoughts away and got to her feet, wandering over to the bathroom.

She ran the faucet and splashed water on her face, taking off the small amount of make-up still left from that morning and then moisturizing her face. She peeled off her clothes and got into her PJ's, before she climbed into bed and snuggled down for the night.

It had been one hell of a first night in town, but she was looking forward to shutting off the exterior distractions and getting thrown into her work.

Her first day on the job was going to be a good one, and she closed her eyes to drift off into a peaceful sleep.

CHAPTER 5

Sean was waiting outside the front of the hotel not long after 8am, his jeans were tight on his hips and he had a rucksack slung over his shoulder. He reminded Pamela of something straight out of an 80's high school movie, his hair was tall with a bouffant and a streak of gel, and his sunglasses were big and shiny.

"Morning," she said, trying not to smirk.

"Finally," Sean said, tapping his wrist, and it made Pamela want to roll her eyes. She wasn't anywhere near late, and she could tell that he was going to be busting her ass from this moment on.

"Okay, so I'm going to drop you up on the mountain close to where the hunters went missing," he said as he slipped his cellphone into his back pocket and hitched the bag up onto his shoulder. I'm going to hike up further and see what I can find closer to the summit. I'll have a radio on me, and this one is for you..." He passed her a walkie-talkie and it crackled with static in her hand.

"No problem," she said.

She hadn't thought much about being up on the mountain alone, but now that it was coming to the point where they were going to head out, she was getting kind of nervous that she would be left in a place where two grown men had just vanished without a trace and animals had been dying in vast quantities.

"Have you spoken to the rangers?" she asked as she clipped the radio to her belt. "This is a national park; we probably need permission."

Sean rolled his eyes and sighed. Clearly, he hadn't thought of everything.

"Seriously?" he said with irritation.

"Of course," she nodded. "I thought you would have known that."

"You're the environmental expert," he said flatly. "I'm the investigative brain."

Pamela shrugged and tried not to laugh. It was fun seeing him so ruffled.

"Fine," he sighed. "Hang on."

He marched back through the glass doors at the front of The Hollow Hotel and they closed slowly behind him.

When Pamela turned and looked around, she was greeted by the most perfect morning out on Main Street. The flowers in the hanging baskets were bright red and lush, the trees were thick and full, and the sun was shining brightly. The air was clear and crisp, and the breeze was still cool, but it was welcomed, as people of the town wandered up and down, doing their morning routines, buying coffee and newspapers, dashing out to get a carton of milk, and walking their dogs. Pamela found herself caught up in the people watching and almost forgot that she was going to have to tear herself away and start working.

When she had been observing them in a dreamlike state for a while, she was suddenly aware of Sean's footsteps coming up from behind and she turned to greet him.

"Okay," he said, a little flustered. "I've spoken to the old broad on the front desk and she confirms what you thought, we do need permission."

Pamela had to resist the urge to gloat, but she just smiled sweetly and let him continue.

"She knows the ranger personally and called his cell, and he said he's going to send us the paperwork over as soon as possible, along with two chaperones."

"Chaperones?" Pamela raised her eyebrow.

"Umm hmm," Sean rolled his eyes. "These small-town folks are so goddamn precious. What do they think we're honestly going to do? We're here to help them, for Christ's sake."

Sean was getting angrier by the minute and Pamela found herself smiling nervously and turning back to watch the crowd. He had such a bad temper when it came to things like this, and it was clear that he hated to be wrong. She, on the other hand, was glad of the fact she would have someone alongside her on the mountain. It would be good to have a person beside her who knew the area, who could show her exactly where the phenomena had started to occur, and more than anything, someone to, hopefully, make sure she didn't vanish like the two hunters had weeks before.

They stood together outside the hotel for at least thirty minutes, and Pamela tried to not notice as Sean became more and more impatient. She opened her notebook and started to make some notes of where she wanted to look first and what tests she wanted to do. And then, when she couldn't think of anything more, she opened her backpack and pulled out her bottle of water and took a long, drawn out sip.

Even though she hadn't drunk a whole lot the previous evening at the bar, she could still tell that she'd had alcohol in her system, and her mouth was dry. It was one of the reasons she didn't like to drink a whole lot. She hated the feeling, the next day, of being so sleepy and depleted of energy when there was literally no reason for it.

"Oh, here we go," Sean said with a drawl as he caught sight of the ranger coming into view. "Great." His voice dipped and the way he sounded nervous made Pamela's heart jump a little too.

She didn't know how she knew, but before she even looked up to see who the ranger was walking with, she had the feeling it would be him.

Her skin was tingling like fire, and her heart was racing, and the familiar pull twisting inside her stomach was working its way out and forward, almost propelling her toward him.

She finally got the nerve to put herself out of her misery, and she wasn't at all surprised when their eyes met.

Ryder was the chaperone heading toward them with the ranger.

She smiled and so did he, but neither of them said a word.

"Hey," the ranger said, adjusting his hat and holding out his hand to Sean. "I'm Dean, the Bridge Hollow Ranger."

"Hi," Sean said. "I'm Sean and this is Pamela."

Dean turned to Pam and smiled, holding out his hand, and she shook it before she let her gaze drift back to Ryder.

"I've got some paperwork for you folks to fill out, just to confirm you're not going to be doing anything dangerous up in our national park or going to be making anything worse. We've had a rough couple of months, and we don't need any more controversy."

Ryder smiled and held Pamela's gaze. She looked down at the ground as her heart raged in her chest. What were the chances of this happening? She hadn't even been in town for twenty-four hours and already, she had accidentally met Ryder three times. She felt nervous around him, but also, there was something radiating from him that screamed protection. Maybe it was because he was so big and burly, or maybe it was because he had a way of holding himself that made it clear he could handle just about anything; the way he looked at Pamela made her feel safe.

She bit her bottom lip and finally plucked up the courage to meet his eyes again. The glint of gold shone bright, and she felt a pulse of heat under her skin and between her legs.

"Do you have transportation?" Ranger Dean asked Sean.

"Yes, sir," Sean confirmed as he pointed to the rental car parked behind him.

"And are you both heading up to the same point?" he asked.

"No," Pamela found herself speaking before she was even aware the words were flying out of her mouth. "Sean is heading up closer to the summit and I need to be where the hunters went missing and the animals have been found."

She felt Sean's eyes on her as if she had just blown their cover. It was clear Sean didn't want the people of the town following them around, but she knew that if they had said they were going to the same place, then she would be the one left alone halfway up the mountain and without any help should she encounter any danger.

"Okay," Dean said. "I'll head with you," he pointed to Sean. "And Ryder, can you escort Pamela up to the clearing?"

Ryder nodded, and Pamela's heart thudded.

Just her and Ryder, stuck on a dangerous mountain…

Oh my…

She swallowed and twisted the toe of her walking boot into the ground. She was nervous to be alone with him, but she would have been even more nervous to be up there alone… or even worse… with Sean watching her every move and criticizing her.

"Okay, let's roll out," Dean said, and Pamela was sure she

caught a glance pass between him and Ryder, as if they were in on something that she and Sean were not.

She looked to Sean, who was completely oblivious, and then she waved goodbye as he gave her a mock salute and wandered back to the rental car with the ranger.

She turned and looked at Ryder, who was standing there with his huge arms crossed over his chest, the dark hair on them wiry and so manly it made her heart flutter even more.

"So," he said with a smirk. "I guess it's just me and you."

Pamela felt herself blush, but she tried to hide it by turning to the side and smiling.

"Yep," she said confidently as she strode past him. "Come on then, we better get to it."

Ryder laughed and followed behind her, and Pamela kept her head high and breathed in and out a few times to calm herself down. It must have been the mountain air making her so nervous and ditsy. Either that or it was because she had a raging crush on Ryder and was trying her utmost to hide it and remain professional.

"We can take my truck," Ryder said as she slowed her pace and turned to catch his eye. "It's parked just a block down, do you need anything from any of the stores before we head up the mountain?"

Pamela couldn't think of anything but her work, even though she knew she would likely be hungry as soon as it hit noon, but she didn't want to delay anything any longer.

"No," she smiled. "I'm fine."

Ryder nodded his head and strode ahead of her, and she followed slowly behind. She watched his shoulders and how broad they were. Even though he was wearing a leather jacket, she could see the muscles flexing away beneath, and it made her pussy throb.

As he slowed his pace and reached into the back pocket of his jeans to pull out his keys, Pamela took a deep breath and told herself internally to stop acting like such a giddy school-girl. She had no interest in ruining her career by being distracted at this moment in time. She had come to Bridge Hollow for a reason and it was just her dumb luck that she had stumbled upon someone she found attractive for the first time in her entire life and had now been around him for the third time in less than a day.

Ryder opened the passenger door for her, and she climbed inside. She pulled her backpack off her shoulders and let it fall into the footwell, and then she tucked her loose hair behind her ears and adjusted the bandana she had tied like a band.

When he slid in beside her and she felt the truck bow with his weight, she knew he was looking at her, but she didn't dare turn to look at him. His big hand gripped the steering wheel and he started the engine. As he put the truck into drive, the skin on his arm brushed against her and it felt like pure heat and electric.

An exquisite shiver rolled over her. From the point where he had touched her, all up her arm and along her back and right down her spine and into her legs. She had to stop herself from gasping. Her pussy was aching and getting wet, and she wanted him to explore her whole body, her nipples hardening at the thought.

She swallowed and looked away. She didn't want him to see that she was flustered, but at the same time, surely, he had felt that too...?

She waited for a few moments and composed herself, as he pulled the truck out into the traffic of Main Street, and they headed toward the roads that led up to the mountain.

Pamela had no clue what was happening to her. But she did know one thing. Ryder was doing dangerous things to her... and she didn't know how much longer she was going to be able to resist.

· · ·

SHE STOOD AND LOOKED OUT AT THE FOREST IN FRONT OF HER in awe. The trees were tall and so very, very green. It was clear that they were hundreds, if not thousands, of years old, and the thought of them dying off was too horrific to comprehend.

Ryder was leaning back against his truck watching her. She could feel his eyes all over her body, burning into the back of her head, and she wondered what he was thinking. She had the feeling that he didn't like her much. There was a clear tension between them. Every time she stared into his eyes, she became flustered, but he also had a calming presence about him, and she wanted to know more about how and why he was having this effect on her.

She looked over her shoulder and he had his cellphone out and was tapping away at the keys. She turned back and set her backpack down, opened it and reached in to collect two glass vials.

She twisted off the top and scooped up two samples of soil from different locations, put the caps back on and placed them in labeled clear baggies.

"What do you think you're going to find?" Ryder asked with a tinge of hostility in his voice.

"I don't know," she said genuinely. "I just hope it's something we can fix."

Ryder kept watching her as she moved around and collected samples from the trees–cuttings of bark and leaves–a piece of shrub from close to the ground and one of the rocks that was small enough and light enough for her to carry.

"The place where it all happened is about a five minutes' walk west," Ryder said. "A few of us have been out here since it all started and been looking for the hunters. Not that I care they're gone, but it's never nice for the town to be in uncertainty like this."

"Why don't you care they're gone?" she asked as she slipped more bagged samples into her backpack.

Ryder smiled wryly and shrugged.

"Never mind," he said under his breath.

His eyes glinted gold and he caught her there for a moment, it was as if there was some kind of chord attached to her, pulling her toward him. She had to dig her heels into the ground and clench her fists. He put his hands on his hips and a shadow seemed to cross his face.

"You two shouldn't be here," he said finally. "You shouldn't be meddling around in all of this."

Her heart faltered and then it began to race ten to the dozen.

"What do you mean?" she asked in a whisper.

He took a step forward, and the hairs all up the back of her neck began to tingle. Her whole body was responding to him as he moved closer to her and she could barely breathe or focus on anything but him and those intense eyes.

"It's not safe here," he said as he stopped and looked down at her.

She could feel a heat radiating from him, something that was powerful and addictive. Pamela craned her neck back so she could look up into his eyes, and he lifted his hand for a moment and before she knew what was happening, he reached forward and planted his palm softly over the place where her heart beat ferociously beneath.

The sensation that rolled through her jolted her, but it also felt like she was riding a wave of exquisite pleasure. A warm trickle flooded through her, from the top of her head right down to the balls of her feet. Her limbs and spine were like jelly, but his hand, as it stayed on her chest, kept her standing tall and strong. A power was passing between them and she wanted to speak, but her mouth wouldn't open.

His eyes burned into her and when he lifted his hand away and traced a fingertip down her jawline, she shivered and gasped.

"What… what was that?" she managed to whisper.

Ryder looked down at the ground and breathed in and out heavily, as if he had just run a marathon and he was trying to recover.

His muscles were heaving, and his shoulders were rising up and down with each breath.

"You're not safe here in this town," he said with a pant. "They want me to get rid of you…"

As the words came out of his mouth, it was as if she had just been slapped in the face.

"What?" she asked with complete confusion. "Who?"

Ryder shook his head and moved away. The second he had left her side, the place where he had held his hand on her began to throb and she ached to have him by her again.

"No," she said. "Don't leave."

He reached into his back pocket and threw down a set of keys into the dirt.

"Take the truck," he said. "And get out of here as soon as you can. If Dean comes back and he knows I've left you here, he won't be happy."

"I don't understand…," she called after him.

She watched him standing there in front of her and she could see the pain behind his eyes. It was clear that he knew something about what was happening in town that she didn't, and he was obviously caught up in it somehow.

"I don't want you to get hurt, Pamela," he said softly. "And while you're here with me, or even here in these woods poking around, you're not going to be safe."

She took a step forward and he held up his hand to stop

her. He was backing away, his demeanor changing. She could see the gold tint of his eyes taking over and they were no longer brown but amber and gold.

"Tell me what's going on?" she asked carefully. "What did you just do to me?"

She felt different, her mind was more awake, and her senses were more alive. She was on high alert, as if she could sense every little thing around her in the woods and as if she could take on the world.

"I need to go," he said sharply. "But you'll be safe for now. I'll know if you need me."

He turned and ran, and she watched as he disappeared into the trees behind the truck and was gone in a matter of seconds.

A cold chill seemed to descend on the forest and Pamela looked up at the sky. It was still as blue and clear as it had been, but the moment Ryder had left, the world felt suddenly dark and frozen.

She breathed in and out deeply and closed her eyes. Tears were threatening to spring free because she felt so alone. He had touched her, right above her heart, and now, it was as if she couldn't bear to be away from him.

What has he done to me? she thought.

She looked down at the set of keys on the ground and bent to pick them up. They were burning hot in her hands, as if his heat was still clinging to them, and it brought her some comfort.

"Something is so weird about this place," she whispered to herself. "I have no idea what is going on, but I am determined to find out."

She slipped the keys into her back pocket and then looked ahead to the thick mass of trees. She hitched her backpack up onto her shoulder and decided it was now or never. She may not have had Ryder with her physically, but she could still feel him, and she had the deepening sense that he was watching over her somehow.

She couldn't explain any of it, but she knew she had to go to the clearing and get the samples. He had said she would be safe for a little while longer, and who knew if she would have the chance again.

She had the drive and courage to keep moving, he had given her that before he had gone. And she wasn't going to waste it.

CHAPTER 6

She threw the keys to the truck down onto her bed as she entered the hotel room and locked the door behind her. The past couple of hours had gone by in a blur, but she had gotten what she had come for.

The forest had been a mess of dead and the dying. A cold place where all she could think of was poisoned earth. She had collected soil and water samples and cuttings from trees, much like she had done in the unaffected area where she had last seen Ryder… before he had touched her heart and done something to her, deep, deep inside. And before she had felt as if she could take on anything.

He had told her that someone wanted her gone, and it was troubling her. In fact, it was more than troubling her; it was all she could think about. How had she managed to get herself into this situation when she had only wanted to help people?

She turned on her laptop and pulled her cellphone out of her back pocket, setting it on the desk. She had no word from Sean, just a text a few hours before saying he was still with Ranger Dean and after he had managed to shake him, he would be doing a bit of further exploration on his own.

Pamela didn't know why but she had a dreaded feeling about this. As if Sean was about to get them into a whole ton of trouble or even wind up hurt. She scratched her shoulder and let her fingertips move down to the place on her chest where Ryder had placed his hand.

It still burned hot with electricity and chemistry. When their skins had merged, something magical had happened, she was sure of it.

She thought back to the way he had stood there in the woods looking at her, his whole body changing in the subtlest of ways, but ways that she could now see and pick up on.

Had he given her a second sight?

Who was Ryder and what did he want from her?

She shivered and had the feeling he could feel it too. Were they somehow in sync now that he had done that to her…?

She opened her emails and looked at the last one she had received from the agency. It was still early and well within office hours, so she found the number at the bottom of the footer and tapped it into her cellphone before she raised it to her ear and waited for it to ring.

The ringing went over and over for what felt like an hour, and then, eventually, it clicked to an answering machine. It was the first time she had needed to use the agency number, when she had gotte, the job after being head hunted, she had only dealt with a personal assistant, on personal terms. After that, it had only been with Sean. The voicemail clicked on and a monotone voice spoke down the line to her.

"This is the Environmental Sector of the US Government, please leave your message after the tone…"

There was a long beep and then silence.

Pamela scrunched her brows up her forehead and looked down at the cellphone.

Had she dialed the correct number? What kind of stupid voicemail was that?

She faltered for a moment, thinking of what to say, but before she had the chance, the line went dead and then clicked off.

"What the…," she whispered as she rubbed her temples.

Things were getting stranger by the minute.

She placed the phone down and then searched for an email address she could contact, but nothing was showing. The only contact she had for the agency was via Sean, even the emails she had sent over the past couple of weeks to the assistant she had dealt with were now bouncing back and Sean had told her she had moved on to another role.

She hadn't thought much of it until now. Nothing had seemed untoward. She was only just getting to know the place and had expected some degree of secrecy… but this was another level.

Something here was massively off and now that she had noticed it, she wasn't going to be able to let it die.

She closed her laptop and turned off her cellphone. She didn't want to speak to Sean. He knew where she would be if he wanted her, and she needed time to think.

She turned on the shower and peeled off her clothes. She had dirt and mud caked to her knees, and her hair smelled of pine and the great outdoors. She wanted to wash it all away and feel herself again, because now, she was sure that some thing strange and sinister was happening in Bridge Hollow, and she wasn't sure who she could trust.

She stepped under the rush of water and let it flow over her. She soaped up her hair and lathered all down her body, rinsing it away and becoming revived. The place on her heart still ached for Ryder, and he was in her head more than ever.

She wasn't planning on letting him off the hook easily either. He had done something to her, and she wanted to know what. She also wanted to know what the hell he had meant when he said that "they want me to get rid of you."

She still had the keys to the truck that she had to return, and she was pretty sure she knew where she could find him. It was setting up to be a busy night in Bridge Hollow, and the bar would be full of excited revelers, and now that she was all worked up, she didn't care about the potential of a hangover the following day, she needed a goddamn drink.

She dried her hair, spritzed on some perfume, and dressed in a pair of skinny jeans, heels and a cute t-shirt before she threw her cropped jacket over her shoulders and grabbed her handbag.

She was going on the hunt for answers.

It was time she went back to Shifter's Bliss.

As she had expected, the whole of Main Street was awash with people still milling around after an exciting day. Some were still in the midst of shopping, moving from store to store and keeping the town ticking over as the thriving commercial hotspot that it was.

She held the keys to the truck in her hand and gripped them tightly. She could still feel a heat to them, as if Ryder's touch was lingering on them. It was almost like she was holding his hand and walking through the streets of Bridge Hollow with him.

When she saw the sign above the door of the bar, her heart raced, and she felt butterflies scatter around in her belly. She felt much more nervous than she had the previous evening, but was it because she now knew that she was potentially in danger? Or was it because she was feeling things she had never felt before?

She breathed in deeply and thrust her shoulders back. She wasn't going to let Ryder drop hints that there was something much bigger going on and get away with it. He had to come clean, and she was going to get her business head on and ensure that he was open and honest with her.

She pushed open the door to the bar and the familiar smell of beer and hog roast came drifting toward her. Her mouth began to water and all she could think about was eating and tearing into meat with her teeth. The sensation took her by surprise, and she had to steady herself against the door frame. It didn't last long for her to see him standing up at the main bar looking back at her, a look of relief and total awe all across his face.

"Come here," he called across the room to her, and she moved quickly inside, her hands shaking as she made her way to him.

When she fell into his open arms, he wrapped them around her tightly and her heart burned underneath her shirt, as if it were searching for his, their skins pushing together.

"I need answers," she whispered. "What has happened to me?"

Ryder pulled her back by the shoulders and stared at her deep in the eyes.

"I know," he said as he swallowed nervously. "And I'm sorry. Come on… there's so much you need to know…"

CHAPTER 7

Ryder led her out of the main room of the bar, and to a large, iron doorway. It was shut tight, but he knocked on it, and within a few moments, a little viewing panel slid open at the top and a pair of eyes came into view.

The music was loud, and she couldn't hear anything over the thump of the beat, but when the door opened, it was almost as if she had felt the energy of the locks turning to let them inside.

There was a boy behind the door, and he had been standing up high on a drink's crate when he had looked through the peephole.

"Hey, Ryder," he said as he moved to one side to let them in.

Pamela looked at him, he could only have been fourteen at most, but he looked sure of himself and completely at ease.

"Hey," Ryder nodded as he ushered Pamela past the boy and further down the dark hallway that was opening out in front of them.

The boy locked the door behind them and then sat back down on the crate and started to read a magazine.

"Don't let anyone else in here for now," he said sternly. "Do you understand?"

The boy nodded his head slowly and looked a little nervous.

"But what if…?" the boy began.

"No one!" Ryder said seriously.

The boy looked at Pamela with suspicion and then he reluctantly drew his eyes away from her and back to the magazine on his knees. He looked wary and unsure of what to make of all this, but that was nothing compared to what Pamela was feeling. It was as if she were being pulled into some kind of underground room where an illegal card game was happening. Her heart began to race a little harder as her nerves started to take hold. She had no clue what was happening, but she knew that she had to see it through. She had come this far, and Ryder was going to open up to her. Hopefully, he was going to tell her all she needed to know.

He stopped by a door at the end of the dark hallway and opened it before he flicked on a light and stepped back to let Pamela walk in first. As she rounded the corner and saw a desk and immaculate office space, she breathed a sigh of relief.

The room was empty, and Ryder closed the door quietly behind her and motioned to a seat on one side of the desk. Pamela sat down and he made his way around to the other side, turning on the table lamp and illuminating the rest of the room.

It was a nice office, and Pamela let her eyes travel around and take it all in. There were large filing cabinets all along one wall, and pictures adorned the rest. She could see images of Ryder when he looked slightly younger, out in a woodland somewhere with a group of other guys, holding up fishing lines with big fish on the end, proudly showing off their catch of the day. She saw images of the bar before it had become Shifter's Bliss, and black and white photographs of the town of Bridge Hollow that must have gone back almost a hundred years. She found herself stopping and focusing on one of what looked to be a mine, with miners all in their work gear in front, holding pickaxes and helmets.

"Who are they?" she asked, and she felt Ryder's gaze travel with hers.

"Some of the original settlers here," he said. "It was a long, long time ago."

Pamela smiled and nodded, before she turned back to him and their eyes met across the desk. Her heart fluttered when she was held by them again, and the space on her chest where he had placed his hand burned hot and seemed to crackle with electricity. She reached up and touched it instinctively, and his eyes went down to it. He cleared his throat and then smiled.

"Tell me what's going on," she whispered. "What is this weird back office, and who is the kid out there?"

Ryder smirked and leaned forward.

"That's just Jerry," he said warmly. "He's one of the kids from around town who looks to earn a little extra cash. Now that school is out, he's doing a few nights here for me, making sure no one tries to get back into this office area. You'd be surprised at how many people in this town have wandering hands when it comes to money and other people's things."

"Really?" she asked with shock. "I never thought things like that would happen in such a small community."

"Oh, it sure does," he said. "Plus, we have a little conflict of our own going on here. Two different sides, I guess you could call it, and I'm sure the people not on my side would love to get their hands on some of the things I have stored away in here."

"The people not on your side?" she asked with a raised eyebrow. "What is this, like West Side Story?"

Ryder's eyes crinkled with warmth and his face cracked into a genuinely happy smile.

"You've got a great sense of humor," he said. "It's much welcomed, believe me."

"I'm glad," she smiled back shyly. "But I still think you need to elaborate. Especially, on what you said to me earlier…"

The words hung heavy in the air, and Ryder sighed and leaned back into his chair. He ran a big, rough hand across his mouth and chin and breathed deeply as their eyes continued to stay fixed on each other's.

"Is this dangerous?" she asked him, almost breathlessly.

Ryder nodded slowly.

"All of it is…," he whispered. "You being here in town, you looking around in the woods, even you being here in this office…"

"Why?" she asked as she leaned forward.

A chill was rolling over her entire body and she had to clutch her hands together to stop them from shaking.

"You've heard the legends about this place?" he asked her seriously.

She nodded slowly, but there had been so many things she had read and heard, she didn't know fact from fiction.

"I didn't know if any of it was true," she said.

"It is," Ryder confirmed as he opened his arms out and placed them on the armrests.

"What is?" she grilled him.

He faltered for a moment and then he seemed to internally debate with himself, before he shook his head and leaned back forward.

"Okay," he said. "I need to level with you because of what

happened. I know all of this is going to sound crazy, but I kind of think you're going to understand it too…"

The spot where he had touched her chest began to radiate heat, and she gasped as she touched it.

"What are you?" she asked him suspiciously. "And what have you done to me?"

Ryder slowly got to his feet and walked around the side of the desk, so he was standing in front of her. He looked down at her and she felt her entire body stiffen. She was nervous around him, but in the best kind of way, and deep between her legs, something else was happening, she was feeling turned on and red hot, and she wanted nothing more than to jump up and wrap her arms and legs around him.

"I don't know what you've heard about our town," Ryder began as he sat down on the edge of the desk and faced her fully, "but you must have seen the various totems and depictions of bears and wolves scattered around?"

Her mind instantly flipped to the statue in the center of Main Street. The half man, half bear… the violence behind it and the struggle. The bear ripping out of the man's body and roaring free.

"The statue?" she asked nervously.

"Exactly," Ryder nodded.

"What about it?" she said.

"There have been legends around here for years that there are packs of wild animals, large animals, ones that are dangerous and magical. It's one of the big pulls for tourists coming to the town, as if they expect to be able to go hiking up the mountain and run into their very own Big Foot," he half laughed. "But what they don't understand is, that these animals are among them all day, every day… right in plain sight."

A chill rolled over her again and her skin tingled.

"Not even half of the people who live in Bridge Hollow

know the truth. Some of them have been labeled crazy by their families because they've had sightings of their own, and some of them don't even dare speak up. The others probably think it's all just hype and aren't interested. There are a lot of old-timers here, and not all of them are so open minded to the idea of things not being quite what they seem."

"And why aren't things quite what they seem?" Pamela interjected.

"Because the legends aren't just legend. It's true, all of it..."

He trailed off and sighed, but his eyes didn't leave hers. She saw the tinge of gold and amber returning to them, and the place on her chest burned even hotter.

"I'm a shifter, Pamela...," he said suddenly.

She heard the words and they registered, but she didn't even know if she truly knew what he meant. She had heard of the legends and she had seen the statue in the center of town. One of the biggest legends of Bridge Hollow were the mythical man bears that roamed the forests and the mountainside, but not only that, there were wolves too. She had always imagined it all being down to a full moon, but what she was seeing in Ryder made her realize what had been different about him all along....

He was part animal... and it was always there, lurking beneath the surface.

She gasped and reached up to touch the place where he had laid his hand on her and done something to her.

"You feel that?" he asked her. "Now, you will always feel it."

"What did you do to me?" she whispered, a hint of anger in her voice.

"Something I had to do to keep you safe." He was being so serious, she knew that there was no way he was lying.

"Why am I in danger?" she asked him nervously.

The tension between them was mounting with each passing second, and she felt herself moving closer to him. It was as if they were being pulled together by an invisible force, something was winding them in closer and closer with each breath they took, and suddenly, they were only centimeters apart. He stood from the corner of the desk and looked down on her with his dark, gold-tinged eyes, and she longed to reach up and touch him. She wanted to wrap her arms around his neck and kiss the hell out of him; she wanted to feel her body against his, to trace her fingers along his incredible muscles and feel the animal within.

Her heart was racing, hard and fast, and she could sense the change within him too, as if he was fighting to keep control.

"My pack doesn't trust you," he said finally, and his eyes were so serious and full of angst she could feel his pain. "They want you gone."

"Your pack?" she whispered.

"The other bears…" He said it, and it all made sense.

Ryder was part man, part bear… he was a powerful being and now, he was taking hold of her heart.

"The people you're working for," he said. "I can tell you're innocent, but they're not… they are not government."

When he spoke the words, Pamela's heart seemed to crash into her stomach. Her breathing became rapid and her mind was racing.

"What do you mean?" she asked with confusion. "I… They must be…"

"They're not," Ryder told her with all the confidence in the world. "We don't know who they are, but they're not the government. They're lying to you, and they're poking around here, looking for something, and it's putting everyone on edge. No one knows who they can trust."

Pamela sank down onto the desk next to him and stared

into space. She thought of what had happened already that day, how she had been ditched by Sean almost immediately. He hadn't cared about her safety out on the mountain, he hadn't known they would need permission from the national park, and he had then gone on to disappear once he had managed to shake Ranger Dean. He had been nothing but secretive with her, and although he was clearly very switched on and knew what he was doing, there was something about him that was so unprepared. It was suddenly blaringly obvious that he couldn't have been part of a government organization.

Pamela rubbed her temples and furrowed her brow. This onslaught of information was giving her a headache, but she was smart enough to know that she had to take it all in and gather the facts.

"So, you're telling me, the people I work for have been lying to me, and now a group of wild man-bears want me dead?"

"Not dead," he said nervously. "Just out of the picture."

"And why did you put it upon yourself to come and help me?" she asked as she turned her head and their eyes met again.

"Because, the moment I lay eyes on you, I knew you were different," he said. "I saw that guy you were with in the lobby of the hotel and I could see how embarrassed you were by him. I have a sixth sense for a pure soul, and yours was screaming out to me. His, on the other hand, was dark and black. He's hiding something and isn't genuine. I was worried about you, and not only that but…" He stopped for a moment and then his hand moved on top of hers.

She felt the heat in his palm, and it made her bones quiver. He was so sexy and handsome, and so powerful. He had the most amazing energy of anyone she had ever encountered, and it was pulling her in more and more. Her nerves were rife, and her heart raged away below her breast-bone. She felt the place on her chest throb with desire, and her hand now was tingling, reacting to his skin, and wanting more of him.

"I knew when I saw you...," he said quietly. "I knew that you were the one I had been waiting for..."

Her heart swelled and her limbs felt like jelly. She had spent so much time avoiding men and love, this had taken her totally by surprise, but she would be lying if she didn't admit that she knew what he meant. When their eyes had met for the first time in the lobby of The Hollow Hotel, something had been awakened in her that she didn't know how to handle. And now she was there with him, in a quiet back room of his bar, and he was telling her some of the most insane things she had ever heard in her entire life, and yet, she knew they were completely true. She felt his honesty, and she knew she could trust him. He was being open with her, and things were beginning to make sense, however out of this world and crazy it all sounded.

"Ryder...," she whispered as his hand squeezed hers, and her heart beat harder and harder.

"Each one of us has one true mate," he said. "When I saw you, I knew I had found mine."

She reached up with her free hand and cupped his cheek. The heat beneath his skin was raw and fierce, and she could see the animal in his eyes coming to the fore. His instincts were primal and savage, and she could sense that he could easily tear her apart, and he was doing everything in his power not to take her right there and then.

She moved a little closer and he took hold of her wrists and pinned them lightly behind her back as their bodies pulled closer together and their lips were almost touching. She could barely breathe, and every inch of her was turned on and open to him. When he kissed her, the whole world seemed to spin, and she was lost in his arms. He pulled her closer, still holding on to her wrists and gripping her at the base of her spine. She could feel his power, and she knew she was completely at his mercy, but she had never wanted anything more.

When they broke apart and looked into each other's eyes, she knew that something big had just happened. The touch to her chest had changed her body's chemistry and bound her to him, but the kiss had sealed them in an even deeper way.

She felt now that she was truly his. And no one would ever be able to tear them apart.

"This is so dangerous," he told her, his breath hot and heavy on her face. "If the pack finds out…"

She swallowed and looked into his eyes. Her nerves rising by the minute.

"They wanted me to get rid of you today when we were up on the mountain, but I knew I would never do it… it's one of the reasons I volunteered to be the one to go with Dean."

"So, it wasn't a coincidence you turned up today?"

He shook his head.

"I wasn't about to let any of the other members of the pack take you onto the mountain. I know what they're capable of when they don't trust someone."

Her blood began to run cold.

"I'm going to keep you safe," he told her as he cupped her face and stared sternly into her eyes. "But I need your help too."

She nodded.

"You have to find out what Sean is up to," he said. "If he isn't government, then who the hell is he? And what is he looking for here?"

She nodded nervously and leaned into his touch.

"I'm scared," she whispered.

"You don't need to be," he reassured her. "I've got you now. You're completely safe, no one can harm you now that you're joined to me."

She nodded, and even though this concept was completely new to her, she felt it deep in her bones. She felt the connection they shared now, and she knew that if she were in danger, then somehow, he would know and come running.

"I'm going to help you get back to the hotel," he said. "And then I'm going to speak to the pack and tell them you've got nothing to do with it and that you're with us now. Okay?"

She nodded.

"I still think I can help," she said. "With my knowledge of the environment, I think I can find out what is happening here in town and what is causing all these strange phenomena…"

Ryder nodded.

"None of us know for sure, but some of us already have an idea of what may be happening," he said ominously. "But we need to be sure."

"And what is that?" she asked, her heart racing.

He reached up and traced a finger down her jawline.

"Take in what I've already told you, for now… it's a lot… while I'm here, your mind is open to the impossible and everything will make sense. Once you're alone, it's going to take a little more to process."

"Okay." She didn't want to argue with him. She knew he was right. He had just dropped ten bombshells and she was still absorbing it all, but her mind was calm. Everything Ryder had told her seemed to make complete sense.

"I feel duped," she said sadly as she looked down at the floor. "By Sean… and by myself. I'm embarrassed; I thought that I'd landed some big government job, when really I was being used…"

She felt tears welling up behind her eyes, and Ryder took hold of her hand and held it to his lips.

"You must not feel like that," he said sternly. "You're clearly incredibly intelligent, they want you for your mind. They know you can help them, but what we are all worried about is what they are going to dig up here and expose. People nosing around, scientists and supposed government types, none of that is good for people like me. My kind and I are in danger as long as they are here in town."

She nodded, and she completely understood. She could only imagine what type of man Sean would turn into if he found out the truth about Bridge Hollow and the shifter packs that lived there. It would blow his mind and then all he would see was dollar signs.

It made her shudder.

The thought of a man like Ryder being exploited and harmed for financial gain was too much to bear.

"I need time with the pack," he said softly. "Until I know I can trust them not to harm you, we can't be seen together."

The nerves crept up the back of her neck and her palms began to sweat.

"They wanted you gone; I have to take certain steps to let them know that they can trust you. It's not just as simple as me walking in and declaring everything is okay and that now, I've imprinted on you..."

Imprinted...

She had never heard the word before, but she reached up and touched the place on her chest where he had laid his palm on her earlier that day in the woods. She felt it pulse and she could feel his energy within it.

Suddenly, the word made sense.

He had touched her and made her his.

She smiled at him and then looked away shyly. She didn't know what to make of it all, only that she had gotten herself into one hell of a mess… but she was starting to be glad of it, nonetheless.

Ryder was already completely worth it.

He gripped her hand and pulled her toward the doorway. As he undid it slowly, he peered out into the hall and then looked back at Pamela.

"Typical," he whispered. "I'm clearly paying him for nothing."

Pamela peered around the door and saw Jerry sleeping soundly against the crate, his mouth hanging open and snores coming out lightly from between his lips. Ryder looked at her and they both smiled, and she was glad of the light relief. The entire day had been so completely draining and now she was on the run from a pack of angry bears.

"Come on," Ryder whispered as he pulled her lightly out of the door of the office and across the hall to another door. He pushed it open and they stepped silently inside before he closed it and another hallway spread out in front of them with a fire escape at the end.

"This place is like a maze," she whispered, trying to be as quiet as she could.

"It is," he said. "And it sure as hell comes in handy."

They raced down the hall to the end, and when Ryder opened the fire escape, the cool, mountain night air hit them and seemed to bring them back to the real world.

She stopped for a moment and looked at him, and he looked back at her and smiled.

"Thank you," she said. "For having faith in me."

He nodded slowly and then pulled her back for a kiss. Their lips met and he pushed her back against the wall, his tongue sliding in against hers and exploring her mouth so deeply that he took her breath away.

She wanted him so badly, and there they were, in the dead

of night, among all the magic and danger of Bridge Hollow, but they were the only two people in the world.

She knew there and then she had found something special in Ryder. She just hoped that the rest of the town wouldn't be determined to tear them apart.

CHAPTER 8

*S*he woke with a start in the pitch black and sat up straight. She was panting and her skin was glistening with sweat. Her heart was beating so fast she could barely catch her breath, and she reached up and touched her forehead to find it cool and wet.

She reached toward the nightstand and grasped at the bottle of spring water she had taken from the mini bar before bed and twisted off the cap before she took a big, deep sip.

She had been dreaming of being chased through the woods of the mountain by a pack of bears, and as her mind started to awaken and she remembered the events of the previous day, she leaned into the pillow and closed her eyes.

She was in trouble.

Big, big trouble.

She took another sip of her water and then placed the bottle back down before she drew her knees up to her chest and wrapped her arms around them. She felt safer cocooned slightly, as if folding her body into a small ball would somehow protect her from the outside world, like a porcupine with its spines standing on end to spear any predator that came close.

She could only think about Ryder and the conversation they had had back at the bar. She saw the intensity in his eyes all over again, she felt the animalistic heat coming out of his skin, and she felt his power and the way he wanted her.

Within seconds, she was hot under the collar and her pussy was aching, but she was also afraid. He had told her so many things, and he was right when he said that once she was alone it would be hard for her to process it all.

She was falling for someone who was dangerous.

He was part wild animal, one that was part of a pack that wanted to harm her.

She shivered.

What had she gotten herself into?

She thought back to the way she had lived her life. How she had always put her career first and had sworn off men since she had seen how her father had left her mother in a state of despair. Her mother had always told her not to trust men, and she never had… So, why did it feel so different with Ryder?

She rubbed her temples, a headache brewing deep behind her eyes. She balled herself up even tighter and willed for some internal peace.

After her and Ryder had run through the shadows of Bridge Hollow, to get her safely back to the hotel, he had kissed her at the door of her room and made sure she was inside and settled. She had longed for him after he had closed the door and said goodbye, and she had found it almost impossible to sleep. When she had finally drifted off, it had been close to 1am, and now, when she checked the clock on her cellphone, she could see that it wasn't even 3:30am.

She had barely slept, and she felt exhausted.

Her phone was still silent and there had been no missed

calls or messages from Sean. She wondered if he knew that she had connected with Ryder and if he was on to her. What if she was putting herself in an even more vulnerable position by forming an alliance with Ryder and the shifter bears? What if Sean was now out for her blood?

The fact that she didn't know who he was or what she had gotten herself mixed up in was the most worrying. She felt as if Ryder had been straight up with her and had told her everything there was to know from his side, but with Sean, she didn't have a clue what he wanted or what his motives were.

For the bears not to trust him in the town, then he must have been up to no good.

And then, there was the question of what else were the bears and the town of Bridge Hollow hiding?

Ryder had told her that some of them had an idea of what may be happening, and yet, when she asked him, he had told her that she had already taken in too much information to process.

Her head was spinning, and she was starting to feel like a fish out of water. She had taken this job thinking it was going to be a defining moment in her career, and now, she was caught up in a war between magical creatures and a potentially deadly secret agency.

She had to laugh as the words flicked through her mind.

This is totally insane! You must be losing it, Pam!

She threw her cellphone across the room and it landed on the carpet close to the door of the bathroom. She had never wanted to be at home more in her life, and she wished that she could wake up from this and it be a crazy dream...

But if she did that... Ryder would cease to exist.

A little smile flickered across her lips. When she thought of him, she knew how she felt. He excited her and grounded her at the same time, and she loved the thought of seeing him again.

When they had kissed and touched, it had been more than fireworks. It had been a life changing energy exchange and now, she felt bonded to him deeply.

She heard a little beep and a light shone out from under her cellphone. Her heart pounded and nerves began to rise. She had been feeling so worked up and distressed, and out of nowhere, her phone had gone off, and she knew before she even got out of bed and crossed the room to pick it up that it was him.

R: ARE YOU OKAY?

SHE SMILED.

Ryder somehow knew she was upset, and he had immediately gotten in touch with her. She held the phone up to her lips and smiled. How could she ever doubt him? Everything he had told her was clearly true.

She looked at the message again and couldn't believe the connection they had. She started to type her reply.

P: HOW DID YOU KNOW I WAS UP?

SHE PRESSED SEND, AND WITHIN AN INSTANT, HE HAD WRITTEN back.

R: I TOLD YOU I WOULD KNOW... I CAN FEEL YOU ALL THE TIME...
   P: I like that, it makes me feel safe.

R: Good, because you are safe. I don't want you to worry about everything we talked about earlier.

P: Did you speak to the pack?

R: Yes. They're going to need a little more convincing, but I know I can get them on our side.

Our...

She smiled at that too, and the way he said he could feel her all the time. She was losing her mind over this guy... She was going to have to seriously check herself.

R: We shouldn't talk about this any further on the phone...

P: Where are you?

R: I'm at the bar, I decided to stay here tonight, so I can be close by...

Pamela grinned. The thought of him only being a block away was the most comforting. If anything happened to her, he could be there within minutes.

P: Well, I hope you sleep...

R: You too...

She placed the phone down on the bed next to her and sank back down into the softness of the pillows. It was reassuring that he had gotten in touch with her again, but she still didn't know what the hell she was supposed to do about all of this. Now that she was alone, everything seemed to be stacked against her.

She knew she was going to have to question Sean, or at least try to find out who she was even working for, now that Ryder had told her that it was in no way the government. And she also needed to solve the mystery of the die-offs, of the strange weather, and of the disappearance of the two hunters.

She rolled over and pulled the cover around her, so she was tucked in tight. She really was in a big old mess. And now, she had to wake up the next day and potentially act as if nothing had happened, have breakfast with Sean and then continue working. She just hoped that Ryder would get in touch with her again before then and offer some guidance.

She closed her eyes and prayed for a restful night. Her body and mind were exhausted, and she knew that if she didn't sleep, she may as well get the first train home the second the sun rose... but she also knew that she was in too deep to walk away.

Something strange was happening, and she was determined to find out what exactly was the truth.

CHAPTER 9

The following morning, she was up and down for breakfast as soon as the hotel restaurant opened. She had showered and gotten fully ready, tied her hair into a neat little high ponytail and was ready to head out in search of answers.

She still hadn't heard from Sean, and for all she knew, he may not even still be in town.

She sipped her coffee and nibbled on fresh melon and pastries while the buzz of the hotel got louder around her. Since she had arrived and it was getting closer to the weekend, she could already see that it was busier in town than it had been on the day she arrived. She saw more people carrying skis and more visiting the tiny old museum on Main Street, which was clearly filled with plenty of information on the legends of Bridge Hollow to get all the tourists talking and excited.

Her mind wandered to Ryder and what he had told her the night before. The place on her chest still pulsated with heat and she knew that even though his claims were outlandish and completely crazy, they were also completely true.

She had been touched by magic, and now she was a different person.

She had been claimed, and even though the thought still frightened her, it was also very exciting.

She finished her coffee and rose to her feet before she slipped out of the restaurant and out the main door of the hotel. She scanned the parking lot for signs of Sean's rental car, and then around the side of the hotel, but she couldn't see it anywhere.

She had been in a daze when she had returned to the hotel with Ryder the previous evening, but she was sure that she didn't see it there. It was as if Sean had just vanished off the face of the earth.

She gripped her backpack tightly and wandered across town to the park in the center and sat down on the bench. She wanted to get in touch with Ryder, but at the same time, she didn't want to overstep any boundaries.

Once again, as if he had read her mind, her phone starting to ring.

"Hello?" she said as she held it up to her ear.

"Hey," Ryder's deep, gruff voice came from the other end and set her heart alight.

She smiled and leaned back.

"Hi," she said, and she was sure he would be able to hear the grin in her voice.

"Where are you?" he asked, taking her by surprise.

She had been expecting some kind of catch up chat, for him to maybe ask her how she had slept, but he was straight down to business.

"I'm actually in the park," she said. "Why, where are you?"

"Can you come to the bar?" he said. "I'll make you breakfast."

"Of course, I can, but I've eaten… maybe just a nice iced OJ would be enough?"

"Okay, babe," he said. "See you soon."

She smiled as she ended the call and had to take a moment. No one had ever called her babe, and it was making her stomach do summersaults.

She liked it…

She liked being his babe.

Shifter's Bliss looked quiet and completely shut down as she approached it from the park and slowly made her way to the door. She had only been there a lot later in the day, and there would already be the thump of music and the scent of beer and cigarettes drifting out to meet her on the pavement. She remembered the first night she wandered in there and how she had seen the bikers. So much had happened since then, it felt like a million years ago.

She waited outside for a moment and tried to listen. She trusted Ryder completely, but she had an ominous feeling. It had been the way his voice wasn't as kind as usual, almost as if he were anxious, and she felt that she may be about to walk into a ton of trouble. But surely, he wouldn't do that to her? He had basically told her that his purpose in life now was to keep her safe, and she knew he could feel her when she was in danger or feeling troubled.

Before she got the chance to reach for the handle, the latch turned, and the door crept opened. Ryder came into view and when she caught sight of his incredible eyes and the huge, bulging muscles, she felt herself lose her breath all over again.

Wow.

He really was something else.

"Hey," she smiled.

He reached for her hand and slipped his palm around hers; his heat was intense and his grip was strong, and she glided through the doors of Shifter's Bliss without a second thought.

Ryder closed the door behind them and then he turned to her and smiled.

"Are you okay?" he said as he reached up and rested his big, heavy hands on her shoulders.

"Yes," she smiled. "Very tired, but I'm okay."

"Did you sleep?"

She nodded and shrugged.

"I did but not as well as normal." She looked into his eyes and the gold was returning. Every time the light caught them, they seemed to take on an extra zing of magic.

"My aunt may have something to help with that," he said as he turned and began to walk into the center of the room, toward the long wooden bar. "She's very into her holistic therapies. Crystals and oils, all of those kind of things."

"Oh really?" Pamela asked with interest. "I've always wondered about that… I'd love to learn more about it."

Ryder smiled, turned his head toward her, and kept his eyes on her as he stepped up behind the bar and reached for a fresh glass. She sat down on one of the high stools opposite him and watched him work. He cracked some ice into the glass, squeezed in some fresh lemon and then untwisted the cap off a bottle of orange juice and filled it to the top. He slid it across to her and placed his hands on the bar so wide it was almost like he could take up the full length of it.

"I can guarantee you, right now, that'll be the best OJ you've ever tasted," he said with a cheeky grin.

"Let me guess," Pamela said as she picked a straw out of one of the holders on the bar top and dunked it in her drink and began to swirl around the ice, "another Bridge Hollow secret?"

Ryder winked at her and gave her a warm smile.

"Isn't everything around here?"

She laughed and then she dipped her head to taste it. The flavors and coldness hit her all at once, and she sipped strongly, taking it all in. It was like a party in her mouth, and it was so smooth and delicious she didn't stop for air until it was all gone.

"Wow," she said as she sat back, breathless. "You are right."

Ryder clicked his teeth and winked again, and then he reached for the bottle and began to fill her glass up for the second time, all the way to the top.

"It's from one of the ranches just a little further down the mountain," he said. "The people who own the place travel out to a family orange grove on the coast, twice a year, and pick an absolute ton to have shipped back. They make two batches a year, and then it's gone. I always make sure I'm top of the list for my order, and I never serve it in here. It's just too good."

He looked excited as he was speaking, and it was completely endearing. Pamela watched the glint in his eyes, and the way he spoke with such passion. He was a man who valued the simple things in life, and that was something she had never found before. The men in the city that she had met or had heard about her friends dating all seemed to be so concerned with appearance and material things. They all wanted the best cars, the most exotic holidays, and the top jobs. They were driven by money and thought success came in the form of an expensive watch on their wrist or a fat bank account.

Ryder and the people she had met in Bridge Hollow were completely different. They lived in a beautiful national park, they loved the land and they took care of each other. And here was Ryder, a great big, burly shifter bear, sitting in a bar early in the morning, raving to Pamela about some orange juice. It touched her deep inside and pulled her to him even more.

She was trying with all her might to keep her wits about her and hammer it home that he was surely going to be trouble, but she couldn't help but fall for him more and more, each time they were together.

He cocked his head to the side and smiled at her again.

"What are you thinking about?" he asked.

She smiled and shook her head.

"I would love to tell you," she whispered, "but there are so many secrets here in this town, I think it's about time I had one of my own."

Ryder laughed, and then he poured himself a glass of juice and downed it in one.

He slammed his hands back down on the bar and leaned in closer to her across the wooden top.

"Okay," he said. "I have my reasons for asking you to come here so early, apart from me wanting to see you... obviously."

"Sounds ominous," she said, sitting up straight, crossing her leg over her knee and folding her hands patiently in her lap.

She had heard the tone of his voice when he had called her and she had felt like something was off, now he was about to lower the boom.

"I told you I spoke to the pack last night," he said.

Pamela nodded.

"And again, this morning, at first light." He kept his eyes fixed on hers and her heart was beginning to pound hard in her chest.

"They are still being wary, and not only that, but we have the problem of the wolves."

Pamela swallowed nervously and urged him with her eyes to continue.

"The pack want to meet you," he said. "I told them I would try and get you here and they could see that you were trustworthy."

"Woah," she said as she got to her feet and held up her hands. "So, this is some kind of ambush?"

She glared at him and crossed her arms over her chest. She couldn't believe what she was hearing.

"I knew I never should have trusted you," she said. "My mother always told me never to trust a man, and I never had... Not once. And then, you waltzed into my life with your tales of animal magic and your smooth-talking ways, and suddenly, I'm feeling as if I have lost my mind. I'm such an idiot."

"No, no," Ryder said quickly as he raced out from behind the bar and took hold of her by the shoulders. "Please don't get the wrong idea, this isn't an ambush."

She furrowed her brow and looked away from him and down at the floor. Her head was in such a mess. She had Ryder telling her that she was in danger, and that she couldn't trust Sean... and now, he had led her to the bar and was springing on her that the very people he was saying wanted to harm her, were now wanting to come and meet her.

"We shifter bears have to be careful," he said. "I told them about us... they know you're special to me and that I've found something with you."

Pamela reluctantly dragged her gaze back up to meet his golden eyes.

"They say they don't trust the man... Sean... and that you could help us."

He was speaking faster and faster, as if he were afraid that she was about to lose her patience and storm out of there.

"I want them to trust you, I know that I do, and once they do too, then all will be well. It won't just be down to me to protect you, you'll have the backing of the whole pack… and then, if things get nasty with the wolves, they won't come for you."

"Get nasty with the wolves?" she asked with a raised brow.

Ryder breathed in deeply and sighed.

"So many things have been happening here, no one knows who they can trust or who is to blame for what is going on. Tensions have been so high, bears have been fighting with other bears, wolf on wolf… and now, our inter-pack feuds have become even stronger. We need to unite, otherwise we won't beat this thing… whatever it is…"

He trailed off and Pamela was sure she could see a tear in his eye.

"I've never been afraid for this place like I am now… but there are dark forces here," he said. "And you may be the only person who can help us get ahead of the game."

"Oh really," she asked as she crossed her arms over her chest and scowled at him. "And how exactly do you think I can do that?"

Ryder reached up and touched the side of her face. He brushed a loose strand of hair behind her ear and smiled at her.

"Whoever hired you knows about this," he said. "Someone is nosing around here and knows more than we do… And we need to find out who. And why."

She could hear and feel his sincerity, and she hated seeing him so worked up and worried. The last thing she wanted was for him or anyone in this lovely little town to get into more trouble. The weather and die offs had been bad enough, what if Ryder and his pack were next? If she could help them, then surely, she should go all in and trust what he was saying.

If she didn't, who knows what she could be contributing to...

"I think I should quit my role and leave town," she said without thinking. "I don't know where Sean is, I haven't even seen him since he went off up the mountain with Dean yesterday. He said he had some further things to look into once he managed to shake the ranger."

Ryder sighed and looked at her.

"See," he said. "Even that sort of information is a big help... but I can't force you to do anything. All I know is, I want to do what is right and protect the people I love. If the pack knows they can trust you, then you're safe here, and hopefully, you can help us ensure that everyone else is too. From my pack to the other packs in the town... and also the regular residents and the tourists. This place is about to explode for summer... we don't want any more disasters taking place."

She turned and looked back at him and could feel the pull still there between them. She had wanted so badly to believe he was a bad guy, to pin on him, at the first opportunity, the fact that he must be like all the others—to want to use her for his own gain—but she knew this was different. The stakes were high. This wasn't some asshole trying to lure her into bed for his own personal satisfaction, this was a man trying to save his family and his town.

Her heart beat harder and she took a step toward him, taking hold of his hands.

"Okay," she whispered. "I'll do it for you."

Ryder cupped her face in his hands and stared deeply into her eyes.

"Thank you." He smiled with a whisper before he pulled her to him and held her tightly. "Thank you so much."

"You should call them," she said as she mustered up the

courage. "The pack. It's better we do it now rather than waiting any longer."

Ryder pulled back and looked down at her again before he planted a solitary kiss on her lips and held her there, wrapped up in his arms.

"You're incredible," he whispered in her ears. "And now, they are all going to see it too."

CHAPTER 10

With the bar being so eerily empty, it was strange for Pamela to see it in a completely different light. At night, when the tourists, shifters and the town's folk were all in there, unwinding after a long day, listening to the live music, drinking the local ale, and eating the freshly barbequed meat, it was as if the little details were all hidden from view.

The walls were tall and rustic, roughed up and cracked, with iron candles holders running around the main level, some with candles in them, and some with melted dripping wax covering the base and trailing down the wall to the floor. The fire pits were big, much bigger than she had realized, and the logs that were stacked in them had been done with an accuracy that couldn't have been by accident. Whoever did it, and she would only assume it was Ryder or Wendy, had a specific way of doing all of them so they matched. The natural light that came in from the windows was blocked out by shutters, hiding the dust and the spilled sticky drinks that were still slopped on the floor from the night before.

"The cleaner has usually been in by now," Ryder said as he watched Pamela's eyes traveling across the dirty floor. "I asked her not to come in today… I thought we would need the privacy."

She nodded and then turned back to face him.

"How long do you think they'll be?" she asked, her stomach fluttering with anxiety and nerves.

"Not long," he said as he sniffed the air. "In fact…"

He trailed off and took a step closer to the front door. Pamela watched him as he moved with caution, how he seemed to be intently listening and all his senses were on high alert.

When he stood in front of the door, it was only a split second before a huge, heavy knock pounded through the wood and seemed to echo around the room and the floors above.

Pamela swallowed nervously and moved back behind the bar counter. She didn't know why she felt as if she had to have a barrier between her and whoever was about to walk through the door, but it made sense for her to at least try and have something she could duck behind should things take a nasty turn.

Ryder reached for the handle and slowly opened the door. Pamela took a deep breath and tried not to panic. As the door opened fully, she was aware of five big, burly men stepping inside. All of them looked as big as Ryder, if not even taller and even more broad. They all had grizzly stubble, were dressed in jeans and leather jackets, and they all carried with them the scent of the forest.

She instinctively took a step back and stared at them all. She couldn't distinguish one from the nother, her mind was a blur and they all seemed to merge into one. She cleared her throat and gripped onto the back of the bar behind her, praying that these men weren't out for her blood.

As Ryder closed the door behind them, and they all stood in a line and watched her, she realized she had seen them before. They were the men Ryder had been drinking with on the first night she had come to town. He had sat and sunk whiskeys with them all night long, they had arm wrestled and roughhoused with each other, and it was clear that they were closer than close. When she had watched them, they looked like a group of brothers rather than friends, and she just hoped that they would respect Ryder's wishes and trust in her.

"Okay," Ryder said as he stepped in front of the line of men and moved in between them and Pamela. "We all know why we're here."

One of the men at the front stepped forward and crossed his arms over his chest, and Pamela realized it was Dean, the ranger. He glared at them both, as if he was already in on something that they weren't. She let her eyes travel around the others and they didn't look happy in the slightest, as if they were already hating the fact that they had been brought there to meet with a scientist who had come to town to meddle in their affairs.

"Yes, we do," Dean said as he stared at Pamela and nodded his head. "And I want to hear what she has to say."

Pamela's heart thudded in her chest and her mouth started to go dry. She had never felt so intimidated or put on the spot before. These men would have been frightening enough, even if she didn't know they could turn into animals that could rip her apart.

"Pamela," Ryder said as he turned and took a step toward her, "is innocent." He reached down and took hold of her hand and held it tightly, almost in an act of defiance. "I know you're wary, but over the past few days, I have gotten to know her. I've seen her working out there and what she is doing… and I can tell you now, she isn't one of the bad guys."

Dean licked his bottom lip and unfolded his arms.

"Dean, you were up there with us. You saw how sketchy Sean was, you actually traveled to the summit with him."

Dean nodded his head again.

"That's right," Dean said. "I did see him, and I got a bad vibe from him from the start."

"He lied to Pamela," Ryder continued. "She was led to believe she had been hired by the government."

Dean snorted with laughter and shook his head, as if he couldn't believe what he was hearing.

"It's true," Pamela said, almost in a whisper. "It's my first job, and I've clearly been duped. I didn't have a clue what we were coming out here for, all I was told was that we had to investigate the strange weather and the issues with the animals in the woods."

Dean clicked his teeth and turned to look at Ryder.

"I was with her up there and I saw what she did," Ryder continued. "She was collecting soil and water samples. Looking at rocks... talking about the environment..."

"And the mine?" Dean asked with a raised brow.

"The mine?" Pamela asked with confusion. "What mine?"

The word jogged her memory, and something started to click into place. She remembered the pictures in the back office, the black and white photographs from long, long ago, of men working outside a mine shaft, holding pickaxes over their shoulders and getting ready to head down into the earth.

Dean looked from Pamela to Ryder and back again.

"Okay," Dean said, "I can tell when someone is being genuine."

"She is," Ryder confirmed. "And not only that, but she's agreed to help us too."

Dean sighed and his shoulders relaxed, and it seemed that it rolled out to the other members of the pack too. All the men suddenly seemed less on edge, and more open to the idea of Pamela being there. They all slowly made their way toward the bar counter and each pulled out stools to sit on.

"I could do with a drink," Dean said as he rubbed his forehead.

"Don't be ridiculous," Ryder said with scorn. "No way are you going down that road."

Pamela looked at them both with confusion, and Dean smiled wearily.

"Been sober for over ten years," he admitted as he sat back against the backrest.

"Okay," Ryder said. "You were up there on the mountain with Sean, what do you think he's up to?"

Dean shrugged his shoulders and shook his head.

"I wish I knew, but he's definitely interested in the mine."

The mine… there is was again.

Pamela felt her ears prick up and she looked across at Ryder.

"Many years ago, there was an accident here," Ryder said. "A mine collapsed, and a lot of people died."

"What does that have to do with anything?" she asked.

"We don't know yet," Dean interrupted and rubbed his jaw. "But Sean seems to be sniffing around there and we need to know why."

The shifter pack all looked at her and she stared at Dean.

"I haven't seen him since before you guys went up to the summit," she said sincerely.

"He shook me off," Dean said with a half laugh. "He played nice all the way up and acted as if he were just doing similar tests to you on the soil and water. But as soon as I dropped him back at the base, I followed him again, and I know he went looking deeper into the forest, toward where the abandoned mine is."

"Well, he knows something we don't then," Pamela said. "Because all this is news to me. All I know about is what I've read on the internet and what I've been told by you guys. I'm as lost as you are."

Ryder nodded and gave her hand a squeeze, and Dean seemed to believe her too.

"If you can help us, Pamela, we would greatly appreciate it, but I know this can't be easy. Especially, when you've been kept in the dark and don't know where you are or what is happening."

"Yes," she admitted. "I do feel quite lost here, but I want to help, of course, I do. I always want to make sure the right thing is done."

Dean smiled at her warmly and nodded his head before he rose to his feet. He held out his hand to her, and she reached out and shook it. His skin was warm to the touch too, much like Ryders, but not as intense, as if Ryder's heat was just saved for her.

"Okay," Dean said. "Thank you for meeting with us. I just wanted to be sure, but I know I can trust you, and Ryder can vouch for you. Let's just make sure nothing else happens around here. Especially, now that the wolves have gotten wind of this Sean guy here in town and are baying for his blood."

Pamela winced. The idea was terrifying. It so easily could have been her.

"Have they calmed down at all?" Ryder asked.

Dean shook his head.

"They want us to fix it and are making threats that if it's not done, then our old rivalries will be rekindled."

Ryder whistled.

"Just when you thought things couldn't get any worse," he half laughed.

The other men all grumbled between themselves.

"If we have to fight them, they won't know what's hit them," one of them said.

"Wolves versus bears, ha, let's just see how that one pans out," said another. "Jeez, we don't want another Lost Creek on our hands."

Lost Creek... Pamela wasn't totally sure if she knew where they were referring to, but she was sure there was another town full of legends not too far from there that had been the subject of a couple of articles online. When she had initially searched Bridge Hollow, it had brought up similar stories of large bear and wolf sightings by unsuspecting tourists and people going missing up on another mountain range.

The men all shook their heads and seemed to laugh in disbelief, and Pamela watched them all start to slap each other affectionately on the shoulders. They were all clearly used to coming together and tackling things as a team, and it made her smile. They were like a big family, and she loved it. It was nice to see something she had never had.

"Okay, come on, time you all got out of here," Ryder said. "I've got a bar to open and I'm sure you've all given Pamela enough to think about."

Dean and the others all started to head to the door, muttering their goodbyes, and Pamela finally felt as if she could truly breathe.

As the door closed behind them, she sank back against the wall, sighed and looked up at Ryder with large, open eyes.

"That was intense," she whispered.

Ryder rubbed her shoulder and pulled her in for a hug. His big arms enveloped her, and his rock-hard muscles pressed against her chest. She felt so tiny in his arms, and so completely safe, that it was beginning to become her most favorite place to be.

Now, she just had to make sure she did all she could to help and find out what Sean was up to.

It sure as hell wasn't going to be easy, but she knew, deep within her heart, that it was going to be worth it.

CHAPTER 11

She walked through town alone and took in the now familiar sights of the quaint little stores and the happiness every person who lived there seemed to carry with them.

It had been an interesting morning, and Pamela had now gotten the trust of the bear shifter pack. She had kissed Ryder goodbye at the door of the bar, knowing she could walk the streets safely during the day and not have to fear being dragged away from real life and into a war that she knew nothing about.

However, it was becoming clear that all was not right. The wolves and the bears were beginning to let their tensions rise. The idea was frightening to Pamela, and she wondered exactly who the wolves were, and if she had even encountered any of them so far while she had been in town.

She stopped by a small, independent coffee house and stepped inside. The aroma of coffee beans hit her instantly, and she felt as if she were drifting into heaven. She had been so overtaken with work and all the complications that had arisen around it, that she hadn't taken time for herself in almost a week.

She ordered a big, skinny latte and took it to one of the corner tables, where she sank down into a big, fluffy seat and sighed.

It felt good to be taking some time out to gather her thoughts, even if they immediately seemed to work their way back around to Ryder.

She had never met anyone like him before, and each time they were together, especially when their skin touched, she felt as if they were being bonded more deeply and forever.

She sipped her coffee after blowing on it to make it cool, and then she looked around at the room of people who were all doing the same. Some were alone, reading magazines or sitting with their laptops. Some were in pairs of two, sat opposite each other and having fun conversations, catching up on their week or making plans on what they would do now that they were in town on vacation. And some were families, enjoying a quiet afternoon together, drinking coffee and tasting sweet cakes and breads from the counter.

Pamela's eyes moved around each section of the room, and they finally settled on an old man who was just taking his seat at the table ahead of her. He too was alone, and he carried a big mug of hot chocolate. She could smell the sweetness of it from where she was sitting, and she began to crave one all her own.

He was unsteady on his feet as he rested the big cup down on the table and then shakily pulled out the chair and sat down. He had a long, white, wiry beard and his eyes were still bright blue, even if the skin around them was dark and sallow, wrinkled and saggy. He briefly looked up and caught Pamela's eye and smiled at her.

"Good afternoon," he nodded politely.

"Good afternoon," Pamela smiled in return.

He pulled a rolled-up newspaper out of his pocket and a pencil sharpened into a perfectly neat point and flicked to the back, bending over the pages so that he had a good view of the page he wanted.

"Hmm," he said aloud, as if he was totally oblivious to anyone else in the room. "Four across, an eleven-letter word for a trying situation…"

He was working on a crossword and Pamela had to smile. She had never been a fan of them, but for some reason, she was good with the answers and had always been able to guess when she had heard a clue.

"Predicament," she said, without thinking twice.

The old man's eyes flickered up to her and he clapped his hands together and laughed.

"Damn right," he said happily as he scribbled the word down in the space and then nodded his head. "This old brain doesn't work as good or as fast as it used to."

Pamela smiled. She could only imagine what it must be like to get old, but she still hoped she was lucky enough to experience it one day.

"I might ask for some more help from you, girl," he said with a big grin. "So, make sure you stick around."

Pamela laughed and took a sip of her coffee, before she looked back to him and found him chewing the end of the pencil.

"New in town?" he asked, his eyes flickering back up to hers.

"Yes," she said. "Well, I've been here for a few days now."

He nodded slowly.

"It's quite a place, isn't it," he grinned. "I've lived here my whole life and I'll never, ever leave. Even with all this funny business that people keep talking about."

Pamela sat up straight and gave him her full attention.

"It's a funny thing," he said. "My father and grandfather

came here as original settlers and they used to tell me all kinds of tales. They say so much happened after the mine collapsed that this place changed beyond recognition… a lot for the better, but some… I don't know…"

Pamela didn't know why this old man was chatting with her, but it was clear that he was lonely and had taken a shine to her after she helped him with his clue. She didn't speak, she just let him continue.

"Yes, apparently, before then, Bridge Hollow was a very different place," he said. "And then, the accident happened, and a lot of people died. Some people left, and new families settled and formed a new world up here."

"That's tragic about the mine," she said finally. "I didn't know anything about it until today."

"Well, it's one of those things that gets kept quiet," he nodded. "A tragic event, and one they all want to stay buried."

She smiled and took another sip of her drink.

"Do you know anything else about it?" she asked, hopefully.

The old man shook his head.

"Not a thing," he sighed. "Only that it shook things up here and a lot changed. But then, I guess it would, wouldn't it?"

Pamela nodded. She took another sip of her drink and realized it was all gone. She leaned back into her chair and waited for him to say something more, but his eyes were now firmly fixed on the newspaper and he was clearly caught up in another set of clues.

She waited for ten minutes, maybe a little more, but by the time she had stared into space and twiddled her thumbs for that long, she knew there was no point in hanging around any longer. He was fully immersed in his crossword, and he clearly wasn't going to be chatting again.

"Nice to meet you." She smiled as she rose to her feet and waved. "Good luck with the clues."

"Thank you, dear," he smiled. "And good luck to you too."

She didn't know why but the words sent a shiver down her spine. The old man was kind and gentle and he didn't have a whole lot to say, but he seemed to be wise and full of thought. She walked away and left the coffee house before she took the short walk back to The Hollow Hotel. She was tired, even though it wasn't even 5pm, and she wanted to have a rest and unwind before it was time for her to try and find somewhere to have her evening meal.

As she walked back to the hotel doors, she wondered if Sean would finally be in there waiting, but she was going to have to wait until she got inside to see.

She tipped the bottle of bubble bath into the flow of water and watched as the suds bubbled up and the scent of strawberries and cream took over the entire bathroom.

She was aching, and her mind was still buzzing with thoughts, but since she had come back to her hotel room, she had made the conscious decision to try and relax. She was sick of feeling on edge, and she needed to implement some selfcare before she burned out.

She had checked her cellphone, emails and messages at the hotel to see if there had been any word from Sean, but he was still missing in action. She wondered if he had deliberately disappeared, or whether he had come to some terrible harm, but she knew she couldn't keep turning it over in her mind. She had to stay positive and focus on herself. She had already discovered that she was no longer employed by the government, her job had practically dissolved overnight, and now she was going to have to re-evaluate who she was and what she wanted.

She didn't want to go home and start again looking for work. She had spent so much time prepping and studying, it was as if she had wasted years for nothing. It was impossible to find the kind of jobs she was looking for, and when she had, it had all turned out to be fake.

The idea made her mad and she had to squash it.

She pushed it right down inside of her and turned back to the tub. The water had almost filled it to the brim, and she swilled it around with her hand, mixing in the hot and cold and letting the steam glide over her and make her skin dewy and warm.

She peeled off her clothes and threw her shorts and t-shirt down on the tiled floor, before she stepped out of her underwear and untied her hair so it fell down loosely against her shoulders. It was still light outside, but the sun was beginning to fade, and she left the lamps off in the bathroom so that it was dark and shadowy as she climbed into the water and let it flow all around her.

She rubbed her wet hands over her face and felt her whole body start to cleanse. It was an incredible feeling, after being so on-the-go and worn out, to have the soothing warmness all around her and bringing her back to life.

She lathered up her hair and sank down into the bubbles, letting it wash all over her and she ran her hands up and down her arms and legs. They were silky smooth and the oils in the bubble bath were making her skin feel even more divine with each passing second.

She sank down further into the water and let it cover her ears. All she could hear was the strange rush of water and air, as if she had held a shell up to her ear, and she closed her eyes and felt weightless.

When she sat upright, she looked at the clock on the bathroom wall and realized that she had been lying in there for around an hour, and her hands had turned crinkly. She laughed and pulled out the plug, squeezing the excess water from her long hair and wrapping it up in a smaller towel, before she stood up straight and wrapped herself in a big fluffy one. She dried herself off and moisturized her entire body, making herself feel as if she had been reborn.

The tension in her shoulders had now completely worked itself free, and she wandered back through to the bedroom and grabbed her short, silky, little robe from the closet before she dropped the towel and pulled it on over her naked body.

She turned back to the bed and smiled at how welcoming and inviting it looked, but it was still far too early to call it a night. Plus, she had the feeling that she would be wanting to head on out into town before long and see what the updates were.

She turned on the bedside lamps and drew the curtains over the French doors, before she turned on the TV to a low volume, and the day's news began traveling across the screen in intermittent bursts.

When she sat back down on the edge of the bed, she was sure she heard something outside, but she didn't know if it had been there or just the TV. When she looked at the screen it was scenes of war in Iraq, men crouched down behind sandbags as explosions went off in a sandy field in front of them, as they clutched their guns and took shots over the top every few minutes.

She shook her head and changed the channel. She couldn't bear to watch it. But when she did and she still heard the sounds of crashing and smashing, she jumped to her feet and moved quickly to the balcony doors.

She opened them and stepped outside, looking up and down the back length of the hotel. Nothing looked unusual or out of place, but she could definitely hear the sound of a fight, and it was coming from Main Street.

Her heart began to pound, and she felt herself shiver.

She clutched her robe tightly at the neck and watched out over the balcony as the sound of men's voices came closer and closer.

She was high up and out of the way, but she could tell the fight or argument was about to spill from Main Street into the back gardens of the hotel, and she watched with wide eyes and shock as the trees began to rustle and Dean and another man came tumbling through. She stepped backward and barely dared breathe. They must have been at least thirty feet below her, but she was still standing there feeling terrified of what was about to unfold.

The trees rustled again, and suddenly, Ryder burst through them, his eyes wild and gold. They instantly flickered up to Pamela and he caught her there, but he didn't even look like him anymore. He looked like a man insane, as if he were about to completely lose control and turn into something dark and dangerous.

"You and your pack have to relent, Dash!" Ryder screamed as he began to circle the two men. Dean was standing with his arms big and wide, hunched out in front of him as if he were ready to strike. He looked like a boxer stepping into the ring, but there was something animalistic about him too, and Pamela could only guess what…

"You bears have been nothing but trouble since this news has broken," Dash shouted back. "And now, you expect us to relent? Why would we? We're the ones who are clearly going to be handling all this shit when it finally starts to unravel."

"We need to work together," Dean said sternly. "If we don't, we're even more vulnerable."

Dash laughed. "All I know is, I want justice for the fact you've been conspiring with an enemy."

"They're not enemies," Ryder said. "The girl is going to help us."

Pamela's heart practically leapt out of her mouth and she pushed herself further back on the balcony and out of sight, but she still needed to see what was about to unfold. She crouched down behind the table and chairs and peered out around them to watch the three men below as they started to circle each other again.

Two on one.

Surely, this wasn't going to be good for Dash… whoever he was.

Pamela practically held her breath.

The place on her chest began to throb and she could sense that Ryder was reaching out to her, he didn't want her to be afraid. She closed her eyes for a moment and tried to calm herself down, and then she opened them and moved out a little, nudging herself a little bit forward to try and see what was happening below.

The gardens of the hotel were enclosed by large fir trees. They were so lush and thick that it provided a complete enclosure, hidden from the rest of Main Street, but for anyone in the hotel looking out of their rooms, they too would surely be able to see everything that was about to happen.

"Back down," Ryder said sternly.

Dash licked his teeth and grinned, and Pamela was sure she saw a flash of green work across his eyes.

She shuddered.

He had to be a wolf.

Dean cracked his knuckles and the three men kept circling each other. With each move, Pamela could sense they were beginning to change into their animal selves. She saw the change in Ryder almost immediately, the way he bared his teeth and held his hands. It was as if he wanted to claw out at Dash and maim him, and was having to use all his strength not to attack him right there and then.

"We don't want this," Dean said. "None of the bears do. And we don't believe you do either."

"It's not a case of wanting it," Dash snarled. "It's a case of honor."

"You have to admit, things have been strange around here," Ryder growled. "Since the weather changed and the cold hit the mountain, all of us have been acting out of sorts. Everyone is more alert, and tensions have been rising. But we shouldn't fight."

"No?" Dash said cockily as he grinned. "I think you don't want to fight because you're all growing weak."

His words were like venom, and Ryder recoiled before his back began to arch, and Pamela watched with a wide-open mouth as the man she was falling for turned in front of her very eyes. She watched as his growls became deeper and more guttural, as his skin ripped open and dark, black fur sprang up in its place. She saw his body crack and change, become bigger and hulking, a monster right there in front of her, but a monster she knew she would love, nonetheless.

She remembered the statue on Main Street, the violence that seemed to run through it, and she saw the same pain on Ryder's face as the bear took him over. He had held on for so long, he had let Dash insult him and his pack, but now, he had snapped, and the beast within him had exploded in the most incredible way.

She could barely believe her eyes.

Ryder was now not a man at all, but a large, black, snarling, dangerous bear, rearing up on his back legs as Dean began to change beside him.

Dash stayed as a man for a second more, laughing and throwing back his head, before he too began to shudder, and his frame began to warp. She saw his nose elongate, his knuckles rip open and claws spring free in their place, his back lengthened, and his ears peaked in tips. In no time at all, he had changed into a gigantic wolf, and now, the two bears and the wolf were about to face off.

Pamela couldn't watch. She buried her head in her hands as the place on her chest throbbed and tingled. She could feel Ryder and she was building up all her internal strength, hoping that he could take some from her and fight the good fight. She wasn't ready to have him taken from her so soon. She was just getting to know him, falling faster each day, *and* he had claimed her…

She needed him, whether she wanted to admit it to herself or not. She may have been a strong and independent career girl, but since she had met Ryder, she had craved more.

She craved him and his touch.

And she was determined to have it.

The snarls and growls grew louder and the howling of wolves seemed to rumble throughout the valley. When she finally worked up the courage to peer over the balcony, she could see a swarm of huge animals all charging at each other in the gardens of the hotel, rolling into the shadows of the trees and tearing each other apart. More bears and wolves had joined, and now, the fight was equal, and Pamela covered her eyes again, unable to watch any more.

She prayed silently on the balcony, as she gripped the leg of the patio chair and wished for Ryder to be okay. Her heart beat harder and the knot of nerves in her stomach began to work its way up her throat. She had never suffered an anxiety attack before, but she felt dizzy and out of her body for a moment, as if she was about to pass out.

The noises kept getting louder and the growls and snarls and the snaps of jaws raged hell down below. Pamela peered one more time over the balcony and she could see one bear and one wolf left, squaring up to each other and preparing to charge.

The bear was brown, so she knew it wasn't Ryder, but she placed her hand over her heart and hoped with all her might for this fight to end peacefully and for no blood to be shed.

She darted through the doors of the balcony and back into her hotel room, slamming them closed, locking them behind her. Her hands were shaking, and she could barely breathe, but she knew that she had just witnessed something that was about to change history.

If she ever had a doubt about the existence of magic in Bridge Hollow, then she had now been completely corrected. There were packs of bears and wolves, half men and half beasts… and she was eternally linked to one of them.

The place on her chest throbbed and she broke down and fell to her knees. As the tears sprang from her eyes, all she could do was sob and thank the Lord that he was all right.

She could still feel him within her… Ryder was safe.

CHAPTER 12

She wrung her hands together and paced up and down the bedroom floor, her feet practically making tracks in the carpet with each stomp as she went.

Her mind was racing, and so was her heart. She had never seen anything like it before and she had no clue how she was even going to begin processing it all.

She had seen Ryder turn into a bear. She had seen Dean turn into a bear. And she had seen a stranger, called Dash, turn into a wolf.

"This whole thing is fucking insane," she whispered to herself as she paced over and over.

She felt tears rise up behind her eyes again, and she wanted to just bury her head under the pillow, but so much had happened, there was no way she was going to be able to rest until she knew what had happened to Ryder.

Her chest throbbed and she knew that he was still alive. She placed her hand over the point where he had imprinted on her and she felt the heat within it. She closed her eyes and focused. She wanted to draw him to her, to feel the invisible chord between them tightening as she summoned him closer and closer.

She jumped as she heard a noise somewhere down the hall of the hotel and she gasped as she felt her heart begin to pound. A feeling of terror began to creep up the back of her neck and she was frozen in place, not daring to move as she heard the heavy footsteps come down the hallway, toward her room.

The place on her chest grew hotter with each step and her nerves quickly began to subside. A heavy knock rumbled through the door and she ran to it, placing her palms flat on the wood so she could feel the energy coming from the other side.

She peered through the peephole and she exhaled a rush of relief.

Ryder.

He was there.

She reached for the handle and opened the door as he rushed through it and swept her up into his arms.

"Are you okay?" he panted.

He had blood spilling from a cut on his forehead and his clothing was ripped and shredded. He had managed to put them back on somehow, but there was no way he would have been able to walk down Main Street. He must have grabbed the ripped up t-shirt and pants from the back of the hotel gardens and slipped them on as best he could as he came for her.

"Me? Of course, I'm okay… all I care about is you…"

She reached up and held onto his face with both hands as she studied him. Cuts and bruises were coming out deeper as the seconds passed by, and Pamela closed the door behind him and locked it with both the chain and deadlock.

"Are we safe here?" she asked as she moved toward the desk and grabbed a chair to push up against the doorknob.

"Yes," he panted. "Don't worry. No wolves will be coming here. This is bear territory, after what just happened, they wouldn't dare."

"Is Dean okay?" she asked.

Ryder nodded. "And Dash… everyone is fine."

"But the fight?"

Ryder winced as he clutched his side and Pamela helped him over to the bed and made him lie down. She ran to the bathroom and ran the faucet to fill the sink with warm water, and then she sunk a towel in it before she squeezed out the excess and went back to him.

"The fight was inevitable," he said lowly. "Tensions have been rising for weeks, if not months, and all of these strange phenomena are only making things worse. It was always going to go down that way."

"But it looked so brutal," she whispered as she dabbed at the cut on his forehead.

Ryder smiled and gave a half laugh.

"That was nothing," he winked. "Believe me."

Pamela allowed herself to smile. She was so glad that he was okay. Just having him there beside her, after seeing what had just happened, was the most amazing feeling in the world.

Ryder laid down and let her tend to his wounds. She dabbed at the cuts and rubbed in antiseptic, before she went down the hall to the ice machine and made a pack to cool his bruises.

"You sure you haven't done this before?" Ryder joked as she laid beside him once he was patched up and on the road to recovery. He could only have been with her for an hour, but already, his cuts were beginning to heal over and disappear and the bruises were beginning to fade. She reached out and touched one of them, and he smiled.

"One of the perks of being what I am...," he said gruffly. "Means I don't stay hurt for long. Magic blood..." He winked.

She smiled and laughed a little as she cuddled into him, and he wrapped his arm around her.

"Thank you for coming to me," she whispered.

Ryder kissed the top of her head, and then she looked up at him. His eyes were still tinged with gold, but there was also the humanness to them that had drawn her in, in the first place. He cupped her cheek with his hand and kissed her on the lips and she rolled into him, pressing her body up close and wanting to be with him fully.

She wrapped her arms around his neck, and he grabbed her by the waist with his other hand and pulled her on top of him. She gasped as his hot tongue searched her mouth and massaged against hers. She could feel the power within him; he was so strong and masculine, and she wanted to be completely at his mercy.

He gripped her hips and pulled her along his crotch, his jeans barely covering him. She knew he was naked under there, and so was she beneath the robe.

Her body was responding to him in the most incredible of ways. Her nipples hardened and her pussy ached for him, she was wet and hot all over, her skin tingling and her hands clawing out at him, pulling him as close to her as she could get him as he flipped her onto her back and dropped on top of her.

He kissed her neck and pulse points, and she groaned with pleasure. His hands gently squeezed her breasts over the top of the silk robe, and she parted her legs and coaxed him between them. She was so ready for him, she had been ready for him the moment they had first laid eyes on each other, but she had been denying it to herself. She hadn't wanted to admit that she could feel this way after all she had promised herself as she had been working toward her career and goals.

She felt his hard cock through the rip of his jeans, and she opened her legs wider. She was soaking wet and aching for him, her pussy throbbing for his touch. Ryder grunted as she ripped at his tattered t-shirt and it fell to bits in her hands, exposing his huge, hulking muscles. It wasn't just him turning into the animal now; whatever he had done to her was ensuring that she was raw and fevered for him too.

He grabbed her wrists and pinned them high above her head with one hand as he trailed kisses down her neck to her chest. He stopped over the place where he had first touched her and bonded them forever, and he kissed it hard and hot, making it pulsate beneath his lips.

Pamela groaned and arched her back, opening her legs wider and digging her feet into the back of his knees. She wanted him inside of her and she couldn't take it any longer. She had been waiting for this moment for so long, not just since she had met Ryder, but from the moment she had longed for love and denied herself it.

This was real.

This wasn't something she could walk away from.

She needed this man, and he needed her.

Ryder's big hand reached down for the tie on her robe and she gasped and held her breath as he undid it slowly and let it fall open. He looked down at her soft and ripened body, and she could see the pull of desire take him over. The bear in him wanted to spring forward, but he was reining him in.

"You're incredible," he panted as she wriggled a hand free and clawed at what was left of his jeans.

She pulled them off, the rips in them making it easy for her to tear them away, and his perfect, hard and thick cock sprang free.

She reached down and wrapped her hand around it and groaned when she felt how wide he was. He was so big, she didn't know how she would take him, but she knew she had never wanted anything more in her entire life.

Ryder grunted and growled as she jacked him over and over, and when he couldn't take it any longer, he pinned her back down, holding onto his shaft and positioning himself right at her opening.

They looked into each other's eyes, and Pamela knew that from this moment forward, she was going to be changed forever. She was already in love with Ryder, but once he took her body as well as her heart, she knew that her future would be there in Bridge Hollow with him, and she was so ready for that journey.

As he thrust himself inside of her, splitting her in two and opening her up in ways she had never felt before, Pamela's whole body rushed full of his heat and her head began to spin. She was in so much ecstasy, she couldn't focus on anything but the wave of pleasure she was riding.

Ryder pounded himself into her, again and again, each time his thighs becoming tenser and his cock harder. She could feel him becoming more animalistic and growls were beginning to escape from his lips, but she wasn't afraid. In fact, the bear that was so clearly lurking beneath the surface of Ryder's skin was turning her on even more.

He thrust, and she felt the pulse of his cock deep inside of her and it made her whole body unravel around him as her pussy gripped him tightly and she began to come. She bucked her hips and wrapped her legs tightly around him, driving him as deep as possible inside of her as she jerked and screamed in total ecstasy.

She had never had an orgasm like it, and Ryder could clearly tell that he had fucked her so good that she was losing her mind. She continued to scream as the pleasure rocketed through her, and as he saw her unraveling, he couldn't hold on any longer.

He thrust into her, his huge, thick, hard cock exploding inside of her. He groaned and growled as he spilled his seed deep within her cunt and sealed their bond forever more. Pamela wailed with pleasure as Ryder came hard and heavy. He pushed himself down on her, completely taking over her body and claiming her forever.

She kissed him and ran her hands through his hair, feeling the graze of stubble from his chin rub rawly at the delicate skin of her face, and she had never felt more at home in somebody's arms. She spasmed beneath him and he pumped his cock into her one last time, as he groaned and grunted, the man and the bear completely satisfied and subdued.

They laid together in each other's arms, and Ryder trailed his fingertips down her soft hips and kissed her on the top of her head.

Never before had either of them experienced such a magical and more meaningful connection, and now, they were each other's for life.

Pamela had never considered what it meant to be claimed by a bear. But now that she had experienced the love that came with it, both physical and emotional, she couldn't imagine it any other way.

This man had come into her life out of nowhere, and now, he had changed it forever.

They cuddled together as the sun set over Bridge Hollow and the night began to roll in. Pamela was sure she could feel more of a chill in the air than usual, but Ryder was so exhausted that he fell asleep soundly beside her and slept the entire night.

She kissed his hand before she wrapped it up in hers and closed her eyes.

She was truly in love.

And she had never felt better.

CHAPTER 13

When morning came, Ryder's cuts and bruises had completely healed, and they laid in each other's arms, kissing and touching, exploring each other again and again, until neither of them were able to go any more.

Ryder was so much more than a man, and he had the stamina to prove it. Pamela came again and again as he touched her in the most incredible of ways and opened her eyes to what love could truly be about.

As they laid together, panting and basking in the aftermath of their morning of love, Ryder suddenly stopped stroking her shoulder and sat up and looked down at her.

"I'm so very glad you took that fake job," he half laughed.

Pamela smiled. It had been such an intense night and morning that she had completely forgotten about the agency and Sean, never mind what she had come to town for in the first place.

"What am I going to do?" she asked him as she stared into his dark eyes.

Ryder laid back down on his side so he could look at her,

and he wrapped his arm over her waist and rested his hand at the small of her back.

"I know I don't want to lose you," he said seriously.

"I don't want to lose you either," she smiled.

They stared into each other's eyes, and Pamela knew what she wanted to say, but she didn't know how to say it. She licked her bottom lip and bit it a little, hoping she didn't look completely embarrassed.

"I have an idea," Ryder said, speaking up before she had to.

"Oh yeah?" she asked with a cheeky smile.

"I think we could all do with your help here anyway, you clearly have the knowledge about the weather and environment, and all that is going on deep within the earth. Why don't you quit the agency and work for us, here, instead? Dean and the rest of the pack would love to have you… you could work for the shifters and the national park…"

Pamela could barely believe what she was hearing. Her hot bear boyfriend was offering to save her from the evil clutches of the secret agency that had brought her to this crazy town in the first place. It was like nothing she ever could have imagined.

"Really?" she asked, breathless.

Ryder nodded.

"We're together now," he said as he reached up and stroked the side of her face. "I love you and I don't want you to leave."

"I love you too," she whispered as he leaned in and kissed her.

"You have a place here at the hotel for as long as you want," he smiled. "Or you can move in with me, it's entirely up to you. I don't want to put any pressure on you."

Pamela felt her eyes sparkle. This was like something out of her wildest dreams.

"My aunt owns this hotel, you can stay for free… keep it as a base, and maybe stay with me a few nights a week too… see how we go…"

Pamela bit her bottom lip and grinned.

"This all sounds amazing," she smiled.

"Think about it," he said as he ran his hands through her hair. "You don't have to decide now. But you know there is a life here for you if you want it."

"Aren't we bonded forever?" she asked him cheekily. "What would happen if I left?"

Ryder breathed out and sighed.

"Well," he said, "I haven't really thought that far ahead… but I guess we would spend the rest of our days in turmoil, slowly becoming weaker and weaker each day until we found each other again."

He smiled crazily, and they both laughed, but Pamela knew it wouldn't be far from the truth. She couldn't imagine ever being parted from him now. She had him inside of her, his imprint was there deep on her heart and soul, and she wanted to experience it all.

"Okay," she smiled. "I'll think about it."

Ryder grinned and kissed her deeply on the lips, and she felt completely happy for the first time ever. She had never known these types of feelings and emotions, and although it was taking her by surprise, it also felt completely natural and as it should be.

"Shit," Ryder said as he looked over at the clock on the wall. "I better get to the bar."

He jumped up and ran a hand through his hair, and Pamela watched him as he walked naked to the bathroom. The sunlight filtered in through the curtains and caught on his muscles, making him look even more chiseled and god like.

She smiled as she laid on her back and wrapped the covers up around her.

She didn't want to move for the rest of the day, and she was determined to get some sleep and recover from the love-making that was now clearly starting to take its toll. She yawned and snugged down into the blankets, and Ryder wandered back through and sat down on the edge of the bed.

"You sleep, babe," he whispered as he kissed her on the cheek. "I'll be at the bar. Come down when you've recovered."

"At this point, that could take some time," she teased, and Ryder grinned widely as stood up and reached for one of the hotel robes that was hanging on the side of the bathroom door.

"It's a good thing my aunt does own this hotel," he said. "Because you really did a number on my clothes."

Pamela looked at the floor and at the tattered pieces of denim and t-shirt scattered around the carpet.

"I think I had a bit of help there," she smiled.

Ryder winked and pulled on the bathrobe, before he moved the chair out of the way of the doorknob and began to unlock the door.

"Come down as soon as you're ready," he said.

Pamela nodded and smiled and watched as he disappeared through the door, closing it lightly behind him.

She grinned from ear to ear and pulled the covers up right over her head and sank down into the soft comfort of the mattress.

It had been the best twenty-four hours of her life.

She had never been happier.

CHAPTER 14

*A*fter she had slept for most of the day, she finally managed to drag her aching body into the shower and began to revive herself. She washed her hair and face, moisturized and put on some light make-up, and then she rough dried her hair so it was long and loosely wavy, all down her back. She dressed in tight jeans and an even tighter t-shirt, which was low cut and made her feel hell-a sexy as she stepped into some knee boots and found a little black jacket to complete her look. She smoothed on some plum lipstick and smacked her lips together before she blotted them with a tissue, and then she grabbed her purse and headed for the door.

Ryder had been texting her on and off all day, telling her that all was well and that the fight the night before had helped ease tension in the town. She had been so surprised when she had woken up and seen that all his wounds and injuries had healed, but it was also exciting to know that he couldn't be hurt easily. He was so strong, and now, he was her protector.

She waved to Ryder's aunt on the front desk as she left the main doors to the hotel and headed out into the dying sun. She shivered and wrapped her jacket around her tightly as she felt the unnatural chill in the air, and she found herself stopping in her tracks and looking around.

The town looked much like it had each day she had been there, but summer was supposed to be breaking, and the air felt ice cold like winter.

She felt a twist of dread form in the pit of her stomach. She had read the reports of the die offs and of the strange freezing in the mountain forests, and as she looked up to the summit, she wondered if it was beginning to find its way down to them there in heart of Bridge Hollow.

She shivered again and kept on moving. She wanted to get to Ryder.

The bar was already bouncing, and when she stepped inside, the familiar smells and faces that greeted her was a strong relief. She was already beginning to feel at home there, and as she walked through the crowd and saw her man working away behind the bar, her heart skipped a beat.

As always, he could sense she was near, and his eyes instantly traveled up to meet her. He smiled and stopped what he was doing and moved out from behind the counter to go to her.

He wrapped his arms around her and kissed her longingly on the lips as he held her close, and she melted into him. He tasted so good. And even though it had only been a few hours, she already felt as if she had been without him too long. She knew there was no way she was ever going to be able to leave him and this place behind.

"Here she is." He grinned as he gripped her hand in his and began to walk with her to the bar.

He pulled a high stool out for her and when she sat on it,

he helped push it in, and then, he went straight to the refrigerators and asked what she would like to drink.

"Surprise me," she said with a twinkle in her eye, and Ryder nodded knowingly and reached for his secret stash of Bridge Hollow orange juice.

He raised his finger to his lips and said, "Shushhh," as he twisted off the cap and poured some over vodka into an iced tumbler.

He passed it to her, and she stirred it a little before she took her first sip. She had never been much of a fan of spirits, but this was like perfection in a glass.

"Wow," she said. "Good choice."

"I thought you might need to unwind slightly," he smiled.

Pamela gripped the straw between her teeth and grinned.

Behind them, the door opened and brought with it an icy breeze, and Pamela shuddered. She saw a cloud pass over Ryder's face, and when she followed his gaze and turned, she couldn't believe her eyes.

Her mouth dropped open and she clutched the glass to her chest.

Sean was walking into the bar.

Ryder's face darkened even more, and Sean moved through the crowd, his eyes fixed on Pamela.

"Oh my god," she whispered, as Ryder jumped over the top of the counter and slammed down beside her.

The other people in the bar seemed to notice the disturbance, and slowly, they all got to their feet and moved quickly toward the exits. Pamela grabbed on to Ryder's arm and he gently pushed her to safety, making a barrier between her and Sean as the bar quickly cleared out.

Everyone left…

Everyone apart from Pamela, Ryder, Sean… and Dean and the rest of the bears.

The only customer left was a drunk who laid hunched over a back table, but no one payed much attention to him. He was out like a light and he snored deeply as a bottle of whiskey hung down from one of his hands.

"Sean...," Pamela said as she stared up at him. "What the hell... where have you been?"

Dean rose to his feet and crossed the room to stand beside her and Ryder, and Sean looked tiny in front of them. He had never appeared to be a small man, but around the shifters, his frame was so tiny, he was almost insignificant.

He held up his hands slowly and took a deep breath.

"I know how this looks," he said. "But I have to explain."

Dean snarled and a growl came out from between his lips. Pamela could feel the bear energy in the room rising, and Sean quickly raised his hands in surrender again and tried not to look too panicked.

"I'm not the bad guy," Sean said quickly. "I've been trying to help you all here. I just had to do it as secretly as possible."

Pamela gazed up at Ryder and she could see he was as confused as she was.

"Speak fast," Ryder said. "We're not one for second chances around here."

Sean breathed in deeply and began to stammer.

"I don't work for the government," he said quickly, his eyes fixed firmly on Pamela. "But I guess you've all figured that out already."

Pamela nodded, and Ryder crossed his arms over his chest, his jaw set heavy and his eyes dark.

"Who do you work for?" Dean asked. "We don't take kindly to people coming in here and betraying our trust, poking around in our business."

"I know," Sean said genuinely. "And I'm so sorry. But it was the only way it could be done without causing too much panic."

"Panic?" Ryder asked with a raised brow. "Do you not think there's enough of that around here at the moment as it is? Masses of our animals have died off… our land is ravaged… and people are going missing! What else could you drop on us that can top that?"

Sean sighed and nodded.

"I know, and I get it. But I had to do what I'd been instructed to do…"

"And that is?" Ryder asked, his impatience growing more evident by the second.

"I work for a man called Ernest Smyth," Sean began. "And I don't know if any of you remember, but the Smyth family was seriously old money, and one of the original settling families here in Bridge Hollow…"

Pamela watched as Dean, Ryder, and the rest of the bear shifters all began to exchange glances.

"We remember," Dean said ominously as he stepped forward. "But they left a long time ago. Didn't they own the abandoned mine?"

Sean nodded slowly.

Pamela felt a chill roll down her spine. So many people had been telling her about this mine, and now, it looked as if she was going to find out why.

"They did," Sean said. "It was Ernest's grandfather who owned it during the collapse…" he paused. "He hired me to investigate it. He heard of what had been happening here on the mountain with the animals and the weather, and he had a bad feeling because he remembers the stories his grandfather used to tell him about that time…"

"What stories?" Ryder asked.

"I don't know," Sean said honestly. "All I know is, when Ernest heard the news of what was happening up here, he called me straight away in a panic and said we had to get out here and see what was going on. He thinks it may have something to do with the mine collapsing… and if he's right… then we all need to be afraid."

Pamela looked at Ryder and she cuddled into him. He wrapped his protective arm over her shoulder and kept her there safe.

"Afraid?" Ryder asked. "And why is that?"

"Because this is only just the beginning," Sean said. "Ernest hasn't told me the full story, but he says it could be big… the weather changing, the animals dying… the shifters having wars…"

When Dean and Ryder realized that he knew their secret, they instantly snarled and stepped closer.

"It's okay," Sean said as he raised his hands. "You don't need to fear me. I'm here to help all of you. In fact, I've been working behind the scenes, easing tensions between you and the wolves because, trust me, if this thing gets any worse, you're going to need to fight it together. You can't be having pack wars when the world is changing before our very eyes and we don't know how to handle it."

Ryder and Dean exchanged another glance.

"How have you been working away behind the scenes?" Dean asked with contempt.

"I've been speaking with Dash. I told him everything I'm telling you now, and at first, he didn't believe me. But he knew he and his pack were acting out of sorts, and after the fight last night, he finally saw that it wasn't like them to behave that way. They would never physically war with you bears like that. He knew something was going on, that there is something in the air or the water making them all act strange."

Dean nodded his head slowly and sighed.

"It hasn't just been the wolves; our pack has been acting strange too."

Some of the men nodded, and Ryder moved back to Pamela and wrapped his arm around her again. She looked up at him and smiled.

"Ernest hired Pamela because he knew that if it was anything environmental, she would see it straight away… but the second we got into town, it was obvious to both of us that the environment wasn't at fault."

Pamela nodded. Sean was speaking the truth.

"And that's why I disappeared," he sighed. "I had to get to the mine and see what was happening there."

"And?" Ryder asked.

"And I couldn't get in. There was some kind of strange force around it."

Pamela's blood ran cold.

"We are up against something serious," he said. "And now, we all need to come together and find out what that is."

The room stayed silent, and the door slowly opened. Pamela watched as Dash and the other wolves in his pack moved slowly into the room and everyone stared at each other.

She had seen the pack war the night before, and she had now seen the aftermath. Compared to how things had been, she could see that the tension between the two groups had vanished, and they were keen to get along.

"Okay," Ryder said as he looked at Dean.

Dean nodded and then the two groups moved closer together with their hands outstretched. They all began to shake and pat each other on the back, and Pamela watched in awe as two magical tribes bonded over a common threat. It was both exciting and terrifying, as no one knew what they were up against or what was to come. But she knew she had found herself a new home, and whatever was going to come their way, she would be there to fight it alongside them.

Ryder locked the doors of the bar, and the music came back on lowly. He opened the refrigerators and pulled out bottles of whiskey and bourbon, crates of beer and mixers, and the bears and wolves drank side by side for the first time in years.

He came to Pamela and took hold of her hand and led her to a booth at the back of the room. They cuddled together as she watched Sean speak with the two packs, and knew, now, that she had been instrumental in bringing them all together. Without her and Sean, none of them would be prepared for what was coming… now, they had fixed their old rivalries, and they were working together for the good of the town and their people.

"I misjudged Sean," Ryder said as he kissed her forehead and squeezed her shoulder.

"I know, so did I," she admitted.

She let her hand find his, and they wrapped their fingers up together.

"There is so much danger here," she whispered. "But I know I can never leave."

Ryder gazed down at her and she saw the gold return to his eyes. She smiled at him and cupped his rough, stubbly cheek in her hand and kissed him longingly on the lips.

"Thank you for choosing me," she whispered.

"No," he said. "Thank you for choosing me."

They slinked out of the bar together and headed to The Hollow Hotel.

Pamela had come to town for work, she had begun her career in an explosive way, but she had made friends and found family for life. She had stepped into Bridge Hollow after hearing of the legends, but she was now a resident there with a deep knowledge of the magic and mysteries that bound it all together. And for them all, this was only just the beginning.

She and Ryder had found each other, and they had found love. They weren't supposed to be together, forbidden by Ryder's pack and by Pamela's career-focused ways… but they had both broken down their barriers and learned that their love was stronger than everything around them. And it couldn't have come at a more perfect time.

As they walked the cold, icy streets of Bridge Hollow, neither of them knew what was coming to them or the town, but they knew that, as long as they were together, they could face it and take on the world.

For them, love was conquering all. And they had finally found their happily ever after.

*   *   *

WE HOPE YOU LOVED FORBIDDEN ALPHA BEAR! IF SO THEN you will definitely want to check out the next book in the series!

<u>Click her to get Alpha Protector</u>
Wolf on Amazon…

OR IF YOU STILL AREN'T CONVINCED, OF COURSE WE HAVE A brief preview…

.   .   .

THE SUMMER MONTHS WERE BEGINNING TO END, AND THE chill in the air of Bridge Hollow was rolling in faster than any of the residents had ever known.

Dash stood on the edge of Main Street, smoking a cigarette and watching the world flash by. His dark eyes scanned the crowds from under his hooded brow. The tourists were still lingering, and the skiers were still making their way up the mountain, but he now saw a different turn in the energy of the town.

This place was getting darker and more menacing by the minute.

So much had happened since the beginning of the year. It was hard to believe that fall was already here. Especially considering all the strange happenings that had plagued them for months on end.

He took a drag on his smoke, exhaled, and then dropped it onto the ground before he crunched it out with the tip of his boot. He ran a hand through his jet-black hair and a small growl escaped his lip. He didn't know if he was tired or frustrated. He had been wanting to go home early and not get sucked into another late night, but as the sun was beginning to fall, it felt as if there were so many empty hours stretching out ahead of him that home was the last place he wanted to be.

He took one last look up and down Main Street. The streetlamps were coming on slowly, and he could smell the freshly lit fires from the bars and restaurants wafting around town. The bars and taverns were starting to sound lively, and he craved a beer and a whiskey more than he had in weeks.

He reached up and rubbed his hand across his jaw. Even though the injuries were long healed, he could still feel the ache deep within his bones. He had been the unlucky one of his wolf pack when it had come to a recent fight with a rival gang of shifter bears, but luckily for him, they had buried the hatchet. They had bigger things to worry about in Bridge Hollow than wolves and bears at each other's throats. Now that the weather was changing, plants and trees were diseased and mass populations of animals were dying, it was clear to them all that they had a greater threat on the horizon.

Dash clicked his jaw and the ache began to subside. He had nothing to fear from the bears any longer, and he and his kind were more than welcome in their businesses and homes.

He turned and began to walk down Main Street toward a familiar warm glow coming from inside a wooden building. He could hear the music and smell the smoke and booze from a block away, and it made him smile. For all the trouble that seemed to happen here, he sure as hell loved his town, and he was determined to do whatever he could to save it.

He reached the entrance of the bar and looked up to the sign above the doorway.

SHIFTER'S BLISS

It was one of the most popular spots in town, but if the tourists and many of the residents truly knew what went down there, he wasn't sure if it would make them want to go more or drive them away for good.

He pushed open the door and stepped inside. It was a typical Bridge Hollow night, and many familiar faces were already inside after a hard day at work. He nodded to a few of the bear clan that were gathered around a corner booth, and he smiled as he approached the bar and saw the owner, Ryder, waiting on customers.

"Evening, Dash," Ryder said with a friendly smile as Dash pulled out a high bar stool and sat down.

"Evening," Dash returned.

He eased himself out of his heavy leather jacket and slung it across the backrest, before he leaned onto the wooden bar top with his thick, muscular arms and reached into his pocket for another smoke.

"What can I get you?" Ryder asked as he stopped in front of him and began to clear away the empty glasses on the countertop.

"I'll take a beer," Dash said as he clamped the cigarette between his teeth and lifted the lighter up to let the flame catch the end.

Ryder had been one of the bears he had fought with only weeks before. But now that they had eased tension between their packs, they had become fast friends.

He set the beer down on the bar in front of Dash, and Dash smiled and thanked him. He picked up the bottle and took a long, satisfying swig, before he exhaled and turned around to survey the rest of the bar. It was a bit quieter than normal, even with all the familiar faces, and Dash was sure some of his own pack would arrive soon to sink a few after work beers. He took another drag of his smoke and tapped his foot against the bar to the beat of the rock music blaring out of the jukebox as he looked toward the other side of the room.

It seemed darker over to the right, as if some of the lights weren't working the way they should have been. The booths that lined the edges of the room all had at least one bulb above them and some along the walls, but there was one in the far corner that was completely dark, as if all the lights around it hadn't been turned on.

He squinted as he kept looking and he felt a dip in his stomach as he realized a man was there, slumped over the table in the center of the booth and completely out for the count.

"Oh Christ," Dash laughed as he took another swig of his beer. "What the hell happened to him?"

Ryder followed his line of sight and stilled for a moment. The pair of them looked over to the sleeping man, at how drunk and buckled he looked, and Ryder smiled and shook his head before they both suddenly sensed at the same time that something wasn't right.

Dash looked at Ryder, and then he sniffed the air.

The wolf inside of him growled and he felt the rush of energy and adrenaline that came with fear and excitement. The wolf wanted to spring free and come out to play, but not for a carefree reason. He wanted to come out to protect.

Dash quickly got to his feet and subdued the growls escaping from his lips. At the same time, Ryder's eyes flashed with something gold, and the sound of chairs scraping back against the wooden floor echoed around the room. The rest of the bears had sensed it too, and they were stomping across the floor toward Ryder and Dash at the bar.

The group of shifters, all bears and one wolf, stood and looked at the drunk in the corner. He easily could have been asleep. He was hunched over the table, his arms hanging limp and loose down by his side. His face was turned toward the wall and his drink was still sitting next to him as if he just hadn't been able to finish it. But with their heightened senses, once they had all locked in on him, the shifters of Bridge Hollow knew this man wasn't asleep at all.

Because they could smell death.

Dash felt the prickle of dread creep up the back of his neck and the wolf inside of him worked its way forward again. His eyes flashed green and he felt the animal wanting to emerge. It was on high alert and ready for battle. He let his wolf come to the surface and his glinting green eyes stared back at Ryder and the other bears. They all looked as concerned as he was, and with each step he took forward, the stench got stronger.

He stopped in front of the booth and could see the shards of broken glass on the floor under the table. His eyes looked up to the light fixture above it and he could see that the bulb had completely burst. The one on the wall had too. SO, it wasn't just simply the case that Ryder had forgot to turn them on.

His blood started to burn red hot and he was on high alert. A growl escaped his lips as he sniffed the air and then looked back down to the dead man sprawled across the table.

He reached out and felt the side of his neck, checking for a pulse. But as he already knew, there wasn't anything he could find. His skin was already cold. Unnaturally so. And he knew then that this was not just a freak accident. The man hadn't died of natural causes. Something terrible had happened. And what was worse... no one in the room had noticed.

Ryder came to stand by Dash's side, and they exchanged a glance before Dash moved the man's head slightly to expose the other side of his neck. When they both saw what was there, Dash instinctively growled and bared his teeth, even though he was still in his human form.

Ryder's bear was clearly fighting inside of him too, and they both growled and howled, as their eyes came alive with the animals within them.

On the other side of the dead man's neck were two perfect puncture wounds, lightly dripping blood.

Someone had done this to him.

He had been murdered.

"What could have done this?" Dash whispered as he ran a shaking hand down his face.

Ryder didn't reply, but that didn't change anything. They all knew what was going on...

The threat that had been coming to Bridge Hollow was getting stronger... and by the looks of it, something darker was now finally here...

GET ALPHA PROTECTOR WOLF HERE ON AMAZON...

www.ingramcontent.com/pod-product-compliance
Lightning Source LLC
Chambersburg PA
CBHW071441130726
47997CB00006B/2183